THE BRONZE KEY

K.M. KING

I

THE CALL

Genevieve.

The voice was a whisper, floating on the air.

Genevieve Regina.

Suddenly awake, Jenna sat up on the straw-filled pallet.

Who called me?

The full moon was an unblinking eye at the small, round loft window. Outside something rustled in the undergrowth. Someone or something was groaning. A sudden scrape against the cottage wall sent her diving under the wool blanket, curled in a ball.

Was it trying to find her?

She stoppered her ears with her fingers and held back the scream that clawed at her throat. Her heart beat like frantic wings of a tiny bird caught in her hands. Her breath came in ragged, shallow gasps as if she'd lingered too long near the castle ruins and was attempting to outrun the setting sun and reach home before night closed in on her.

Her mother's stern voice suddenly echoed in her head.

"Jenna, ye have got to curb that mind of yorn, always making up wild stories and such. Put your mind ta sleep with the rest of ye, or I'll tell your Pa to burn that fairy tale book. See what comes from teaching a girl child to read!"

She eased her hands away from her ears and tried to identify the hidden things of the night.

The newly leafed-out branches of maple trees were rustling fiercely in the wind. *Yes, the wind was high.* It was the ancient oak in the dooryard which creaked and groaned, its branches swaying, one occasionally scraping the cottage wall.

No unseen creature. No threatening being.

Jenna's heart slowed from its runaway pace.

That steady thump? *Oh, it's only the front gate.* Someone forgot to latch it. *Probably me!* That long, low moaning sound: hoooo-hoooo, hoooo-hoooo. That's just the slow cry of an owl.

She took a deep breath and pulled the cover off her head. The soft snores of her older brothers Abram and Thomas filtered through the curtain dividing their sleeping space. In the alcove below, her oldest brother, Joshua, groaned as he turned over in his new rope bed. After two years as an apprentice in their father's clay tile workshop, he'd been granted a walled-off space of their parents' sleeping area. Her youngest brother, Peter, slept on a trundle bed next to his parents.

Jenna knew she was too old to be afraid of the night. She was thirteen, after all. Yet so many nights she was startled awake from a restless sleep by something creeping into her murky dreams. Something watching, something waiting. Something too frightening to speak of in the daytime.

She never had spoken of it. Not to her mother or father or brothers.

Genevieve Regina.

Jenna sat up suddenly, gasping. That voice again. Soft, yet urgent. A woman's voice.

Only her mother called her by her full name. And only when Jenna neglected some chore because her mind was filled with imaginings of the kings, queens, knights, and ladies-in-waiting who once dwelt in the tumbled down castle. Or when she was mentally lying on the sweet-scented grass next to the burbling stream near the ruins, watching the butterflies skip across the jack-in-the-pulpits.

The only place she ever felt fully rested.

But it wasn't her mother calling now. It was a young woman. Pleading. Needing help. But why was she outside in the dark?

Jenna never went outside in the dark.

Though she loved the stars, she would not join her brothers to play hide and seek after sunset. Instead, she sat within the splay of light spilling from the open door, entertaining Peter with stories about mythic heroes who dwelt in the star-spattered dome. Or shared the treasures she gathered on her walks—partially-opened cocoons, clusters of wild flowers, odd-shaped stones from the creek.

The dark was dangerous—full of unseen, menacing things, like her dreams. Yet out there in the dark was a young woman who needed her.

Gathering courage from some untapped well, Jenna crept to the ladder at the edge of the loft on hands and knees, as silent as the mice that scampered in the barn. Stealthily she eased her way down.

The moonlight, streaming through the small casement windows, lay in puddles on the wide plank floor. The April nights were warm enough to leave the shutters open, but still cold enough to make her shiver in her knee length nightdress and bare feet as she took one cautious step after the other toward the door.

Fully awake now, she wondered if the call had been part of her dream.

Are you still there? Jenna asked wordlessly.

As she reached for the latch, the voice replied, *Yes. Yes. I'm waiting.* The door swung open soundlessly on well-oiled hinges, and Jenna stepped out onto the stoop.

The night lay silent and still, everything touched with silver. Almost like fairy dust. To the east, distant hills lay like deep purple lumps on the horizon. The lines of hedges along the northern border of their small farm were spiky black walls.

To her left, a post-and-rail fence surrounded a small dirt patch in front of the small barn that housed the cow, mare, pigs, and chickens. On a rise above the barn, Papa's workshop and kiln perched near the woods. Each building, each tree, each hedge cast a deeply shaded patch of black on moonlit ground.

Anything could be hidden in those unlit spaces.

To her right, beyond the low hedges, tiny green shoots peeked up from mounded rows of dirt in the garden. Jenna stepped down onto the frosty ground, walked the few paces to the front gate that swung in the night breeze. She grasped the twined rope closure, about to secure the gate, when the voice froze her in mid-action.

Please, the woman said, *I've been here for so long. You're the only one who can help.*

The plea seemed to be coming from nowhere and every-where. Jenna's stomach churned like cream turning into butter as she replied in her mind, *Where are you?* Holding her breath, she leaned against the gate, about to ease it open and step into the lane leading to the village road.

"Jenna!" A deep male voice sounded at her ear. Jenna spun, a startled gasp tumbling from her mouth. Two powerful hands grabbed her shoulders.

"What are you doing out here?" her father's voice demanded. He shook her gently.

She looked at his bare feet then at his weathered face.

"I... I... I don't know."

How could she explain?

At breakfast, Jenna made swirls and patterns with her wooden spoon in her porridge, watching the rich, sweet cream run into the gullies like the sparkling water of her favorite brook running in rivulets around fallen twigs. In her mind, she was near the castle's tumbled-down towers, weaving a crown from the willow's overhanging branches, strutting about like a princess.

"Genevieve Regina."

Jenna dropped her spoon, sitting upright with a quick indrawn breath, then let out a long, slow exhale as she realized it was her mother speaking, not the voice in the night.

"Oh, you're in traaaa... ble," Abram taunted with a bump against her shoulder.

"Hush, Abram," Jacob snapped.

Jenna blinked at her father's unusually harsh tone then hesitantly responded to her mother.

"Yes, Mama?"

Of course, her father must have told her mother about finding Jenna outside in the middle of the night. Jenna had been unable to say more than, "I don't know," to her father's repeated question of what she was doing. How could she tell him about hearing a voice calling her? He'd think she'd gone soft in the head.

They had returned to the house quietly. She had scurried back up to the loft, sleeping fitfully till dawn.

Her mother's sigh spoke of impatience tinged with tenderness. "I have a special task for you and Abram today. I'm sending the both a you up the mountain ta Annie, the goatherd's wife."

Jenna thought of the long cart ride across the valley and into the mountains, her shoulders drooping. "Do I really need to go along with Abram, Mama? It's so far."

She longed to rest in the sheltering shade of her willow tree and listen to the soothing daytime sounds: squirrels rustling in the underbrush, adding to their winter's store; bees buzzing in the honeysuckle, spreading pollen from flower to flower; branches creaking high above her, stirred by the passing breeze.

"Jenna, none of your backtalk." Her father's rare scolding of his only daughter silenced the whole table and brought tears to Jenna's eyes.

"Now, Jacob," her mother countered in a soothing voice, "Ye can see Jenna didn't sleep well and isn't quite herself."

"Aye, Rachel, that be true," Jacob replied in a softer tone.

Jenna felt comforted until Rachel continued.

"I've made up a basket of cakes for Annie as some of her husband's young kin are visiting from the city. And, mind ye, I need some of Annie's herbs and such. Time you learnt to call on a neighbor, womanly like. Abram will be in charge of fetching a goat and learning the number of tiles Annie's wanting fer her drying kiln."

"Mama, can't Abram just put the basket in the cart and give it to Annie?" *It'll be bad enough to go all that way, but then I'll have to make polite conversation with people I've never met.*

"If she doesn't want to go, I'll go," Thomas piped up. "I can do the proper greeting in her place." He stood up and made an awkward curtsey to Abram, who burst out laughing.

Peter, not to be left out, did the same. Joshua smiled in amusement at his younger brothers.

"Thomas, sit. Finish your breakfast." Jacob was clearly not amused. "You're expected at the cooper's shop." Thomas plunked back down, showing sudden interest in the table's wood grain.

In a gentler tone, Jacob added, "Peter, feed the chickens if you're done with your porridge."

Little Peter skipped off toward the barn.

Jacob looked down the table at Jenna. "You're a might bit pale, Jenna. The sunshine will do you good."

"Aye, Papa," she muttered, frowning at her breakfast.

Her mother made Jenna change into a fresh apron and insisted on brushing her wavy, unruly hair. "Where ye got this mass of raven colored hair, 'tis a mystery to me," Rachel muttered as she tied it back with a thin red ribbon. "Nor this willowy height 'o yorn, as tall as your brothers you are."

All her brothers and her mother had hair the color of fading straw and were on the stocky side. "Ye must ha got your looks from your father's kin," her mother went on.

"Papa does have hair more like mine," Jenna agreed, wondering not for the first time what her father's family was like. She knew he had but an aunt in the distant city of Westerfordshire, having lost his parents at a young age. But her father never spoke of his growing up years.

Before long, Jenna was seated next to Abram on the two-wheeled cart, clutching the basket, a light shawl around her shoulders. Abram, in high spirits at an opportunity to escape farm chores, whistled merrily as he directed the mare.

Jenna stared through bleary eyes as the valley passed by, trying to conjure up the voice from the previous night. Had she really heard it? Or was it just part of a dream? Or formed out of the wild mind her mother accused her of having?

But it wasn't long before the fresh spring breeze playing in the nearby grasses brightened her spirits. As the road took a tilt upward, Jenna heard the wind sing, "Come play with us. Come dance on the hill."

Forgetting her exhaustion, she whispered, "Yes, I'll play with you."

The wind teased, "Chase us, chase us," because the wind is always more than one.

Jenna thrust the basket into Abram's arms then jumped down from the cart.

"Jenna," Abram shouted in alarm. "What are you doing?"

"I'm going to run the rest of the way. I'll meet you there," she called over her shoulder, and ran uphill after the wind, her arms wide, laughing out loud. It wasn't long before a branch pulled the ribbon out of her hair, which tumbled in disarray around her shoulders. When she reached the top of a rise, she paused momentarily to catch her breath.

"Jenna," the wind taunted from a nearby grove of oak trees, "Here we are. See? See us bend the branches."

Jenna ran in among the trees, shouting into the branches, "I caught you; I caught you."

Much to her surprise, the wind replied in a boy's voice, "But I wasn't running from you."

What was this? The wind always spoke in a breathy sigh or huffy gust. Never in a human-sounding voice. Then to her shock a wood sprite landed with a *whumpf* beside her.

"Hi," the wood sprite said.

Jenna scurried backwards into the trunk of the tree, then scampered behind it, peeking around to watch from a safe distance, waiting for the magical being to disappear or turn into a puff of smoke.

But it did neither. Instead, it kept talking.

"My name is Daniel. You know, like the prophet thrown into the lion's den in the Old Testament. What's your name?"

Jenna stared at the wood sprite, unblinking, although she knew it wasn't polite. Its blonde hair and blue eyes were unexpected. She thought wood sprites would have dark hair, deep brown eyes like hers, and a more elfish name. Like Aldon. Or Haldir.

"You're not a wood sprite!" She accused him. "I don't think you're a prophet, either."

"A wood sprite?" He chuckled. "My father would say I have a wooden head, but this would be a new one for him. A wood sprite?" He began laughing so hard he started to cough.

Jenna was so disappointed he was a mere boy that she walked away.

"Wait, what's your name?" he called between coughs, then ran to catch up with her.

"Genevieve Regina." She said her full name in a rush as he halted in front of her.

His smile seemed to tease her.

"Don't laugh! That's my given name! I was named for a long-ago ancestor from France and for the Blessed Virgin. Regina means queen," she replied in a rush, using her mother's explanation for the fanciful name.

"It's quite regal, my ladyship." The wood-sprite-turned-boy made a sweeping bow. "Very pleased to meet you, Genevieve of the Trees."

Jenna snorted. "You're making fun of me. And it's really just Jenna. Plain old Jenna."

"I'm not making fun of you. Honest. Shall I take an oath?"

"Don't mock oath taking."

"Oooh, she's an upright young ladyship."

Jenna glared at the boy. He appeared to be about Thomas' age, who had turned fifteen in February, the month before Abram was fourteen.

"What are you doing out here in the grove, besides running after wood sprites?" he asked, his eyes full of merriment.

She held back a smile, unwilling to show how his charm was chipping away at her pique. "I was chasing the wind," Jenna explained, as if it were an ordinary thing to do.

"Wood sprites and the wind—don't you play with humans?"

"Well, I've only brothers. One of my tasks is to amuse little Peter. He's four. My older brothers' way of playing is to tie me up to the laundry pole and pretend they're wild savages. Mama says they're too old to play, anyway, as they're nearly young men."

She suddenly remembered her task. "Oh my! I'm supposed to take the basket to Annie, the goatherd's wife, for some visiting relation." She brushed the grass and leaves off her best dress, a pale pink frock, and tightened the strings of her white apron.

With another bow, the boy said, "At your service, madam."

Jenna smirked. "What service do I need that *you* can render?"

"Why, Genevieve of the Trees, before your very eyes is one of the relations who is visiting the goatherd and his wife. I shall escort you to the family abode."

Jenna eyed him critically. *At least he's not like the miller's son who follows me calling, "Please don't leave, Genevieve."*

"I know the way," she replied with a toss of her head, not willing to show how amusing she found him.

"But I know a short cut. Come, this way."

He set off, and after a moment's hesitation, she followed him uphill.

"For a city boy, you find your way quite well in the woods," she called after him. "Even I would have struggled to find this path."

He stopped and waited for her. "How do you know I'm a city boy?"

"Your speechifying and your manners give you away."

"Ah, well, apparently I've learned country ways well enough to be mistaken for a wood sprite." He winked at her.

"Don't you have chores?" she asked, ignoring his merry jibe.

"Oh yes, and my studies."

"Oh, your studies?" She thought that an odd word for schooling. Unlike most of the village children, Jenna and her brothers knew how to read and write and calculate, because during the long winter nights, Jacob instructed them in their letters, numbers, and words.

"Why *are* you here on the mountain? Can't you do your studies in the city?" Jenna asked.

He chuckled. "I was ill for a while, and my mother and father thought the country air would do me good. They sent me for the winter and come spring my younger brother Will joined me. He's taken up goat herding, and he and Annie's husband, Ezra, and their son, Naaman, spend most of the time up on the mountain chasing the goats."

He started up the hill again.

"Why aren't you chasing the goats?"

Over his shoulder he said, "I've been given the task of becoming well. I'm allowed to roam around as I please and am commanded to drink all the goat's milk that I can possibility stomach." He jumped up and down. "See, don't I look fit?"

"You look like you're having a fit." She finally smiled at him, won over by his silliness, and followed him up through the woods.

After some time he said, "Here we are," pointing to a small, thrush-roofed cottage in a clearing ahead. The old mare, still hitched to the cart, was chewing contentedly at a pile of hay.

"Oh, no, Abram got here before me, and I'm supposed to be the one to give the basket."

"It's all right." Daniel grabbed her hand and pulling her along, burst into the cottage. "Cousin Annie, Cousin Annie," he called, then came to an abrupt halt.

Jenna nearly plowed into him. The basket sat on the table in front of Annie and Abram, who looked up, startled.

Daniel grabbed the basket and dragged her back out the door. "Here," he said, shoving the basket in her arms. "Now knock," he commanded, then closed the door in her face.

Jenna blinked her eyes rapidly, speechless. What to make of such an unpredictable boy? When a moment passed and she didn't knock, he flung open the door and said in a loud voice filled with cheerful surprise, "Why Cousin Annie, look who we have here. Our neighbor down the hill, young Genevieve Regina, and she's brought you a basket on this fine spring day."

Jenna gazed past Daniel to Abram, who stared at Daniel as if he had grown a second head.

Annie's round face broke into a welcoming smile. "Ah, Jenna, 'tis nice to see you again. Your mother's a kind woman, to be sending such a treat." She chuckled. "Don't mind young master Daniel. He acts the fool half the time. At least Will knows how to be sensible."

"Abram," Annie continued, "this is Daniel, who is the older son of my husband's cousin. Daniel, this is Abram, one of the tile maker's sons. He's got quite a family."

"I know," Daniel said, with surprising certainty.

"How do you know?" Jenna asked defiantly.

"Well, I told you the only job I've had all this winter and spring was to roam around at my will. And my will has taken me up and down the mountain, so I've seen your place and all your family." He frowned a moment, then began to list them. "There's the oldest one. He is tall and thin and is always chopping wood for the kiln."

"That's Joshua!" Abram exclaimed.

"Then there's one betwixt Joshua and you, Abram. He's always ordering the chickens around like he was their captain and calls them his 'mates.'"

"Thomas!" Abram shouted gleefully. "He thinks he's going to go to sea instead of be a cooper's apprentice. I'm going to be apprenticed to the smithy next year when I'm fifteen."

Jenna was beginning to think Daniel *was* a prophet to know so much about her family.

"Who else is there, Master Daniel?" she asked with a hint of sarcasm.

"There's you, Genevieve of the Trees. You chase the wind."

Abram hooted at this apt description of his sister.

"And then there's the little boy, who's always running after you shouting, 'Story! Story!'"

"Peter!" Abram declared.

"And of course, your father, the tile maker, and your mother."

Jenna shook her head. "How do you know all of this, Daniel?"

Her new acquaintance grinned. "I climb trees and spy on people. Comes in handy."

"Jolly good!" Abram exclaimed.

"And he's had nigh onto half a year to hear all my tales about you that dwell down there in the valley," Annie added, looking with pleasure into the basket. After she exclaimed over the contents, she put her hands on her wide hips and commanded, "Now then, young Daniel, go and tell Ezra to give you a good milking goat."

"Yes, Mama said goat's milk is just what Jenna needs."

"What?" Jenna looked at her brother in embarrassment. "What for?"

Abram reddened. "Well, ah, she said you're tired a lot, and, ah, you sleep so restlessly."

"Goat's milk is a great boon for one's stamina," Daniel interjected. "Just look what it's done for me." He ran in place to demonstrate while Jenna realized that her family knew about her sleepless nights. Thank goodness they didn't know about her dark, shadowy dreams.

"Want to walk with me up the mountain?" Daniel asked, drawing her attention.

"What about Abram?"

"He can come too, if he wants."

But Abram was content to chatter away to the goatherd's wife, telling her his plans to be a soldier, if he could only convince his father it was a better choice than blacksmithing.

As they left the cabin, Daniel handed Jenna a walking stick and took one himself. Jenna noticed finely executed carvings of birds and trees.

"Daniel, who did these beautiful carvings?"

He beamed with pride.

"I didn't know you were a woodcarver as well as a wood sprite!"

"Well," he explained, "in the wintertime, there isn't much for a goatherd to do except take hay into the barn for the goats and sit by the fire and whittle on wood. Ezra said I have an eye for the wood, just that my hand needs practice. My father sells them in his shop."

The winding path that led to the high mountain meadow was steep, and Jenna was glad for the aid of a walking stick. Occasionally Daniel stopped, exclaiming he was tired or the rucksack rubbed against shoulders. Jenna knew he was giving her excuses to rest. She was touched by his thoughtfulness and was content to stretch out under a tree while Daniel spoke of his life in the city of Westerfordshire, further down along the coast in the lowlands.

"That's where my father grew up!" Jenna exclaimed. "His Aunt Myra still lives there, but we've never been to visit, so I've never met her."

"You'll have to come and visit my family. I have two older sisters, one married."

"Are you going to be a shopkeeper like your father?"

"Everyone thinks I am," Daniel replied with a huff.

"Doesn't sound like everyone is certain," Jenna said softly.

"I don't want to be a shopkeeper. I'm like your brother Thomas who'd choose to be a sailor rather than the cooper as his father thinks."

"Thomas is just full of airy dreams."

"Is that so bad?" Daniel sighed heavily.

"Well, what do you want to be, then?"

"I want to be a storyteller!"

"Daniel, gypsies are storytellers. You aren't a gypsy."

"No, but there are people who write books, tell stories on paper."

Jenna thought of the few books she had read. "But no one makes a trade at such a thing, do they?"

"There are. Truly. If I can't, I'd want to be a bookbinder so I can at least work with books."

"Or a printer?" Jenna had never seen a printer, but she had heard of such things.

"Yes, or a printer. We have two in Westerfordshire."

"I can't imagine a place large enough to have a printer, let alone two."

It was nearly noon when they reached the high meadow. They found the goatherd, his son, and Daniel's brother, all sitting under a tree, eating bread and cheese. They were delighted with the share of Rachel's baked goods that Annie had sent and invited Daniel and Jenna to share their noonday meal. Daniel and Will bantered continuously, amusing Jenna with their good-natured teasing.

After lunch, Ezra picked out a nanny goat whose baby bleated pitifully as he led her away.

"Can't we take the wee one, too?" Jenna asked, her heart touched by the abandoned kid.

"He's about weaned and won't need his mother's milk," Ezra explained. "He'll be fine."

He turned the nanny goat over to Daniel, adding a rope halter. "Hold tight ta her, Daniel; she'll be stubborn."

Going down the mountain was much quicker, and they made fewer stops for if they rested, the goat would balk at starting again. Annie rewarded them with an afternoon treat of tea and scones.

When they made ready to leave, Jenna sat in the cart, and Abram tied the goat next to her so it wouldn't jump out. Daniel said he'd ride along to the bottom of the mountain and clambered up with Abram.

Jenna felt sorry for the mama goat who continued to bleat sorrowfully and tried to calm it by holding and petting it. She listened as Abram asked Daniel endless questions about the city, the soldiers and sailors who lived there, and what Daniel's life was like there. When Daniel climbed down from his seat after the path leveled off, he waved them on, a forlorn look on his face.

"Come visit us," Abram called, and Daniel's face lit up.

Jenna nodded in agreement. "Yes, Daniel, come visit us and tell us stories. Come soon."

As the cart jostled away Jenna thought, *Maybe he's someone I could tell about the voice I heard calling me last night. He wouldn't laugh at me.*

But for now, she would keep it secret, for it was even more disquieting than the murky nighttime dreams whose feeling of dread lingered long into the day.

2

A VISITOR

The days wore on and April became May. To Jenna's disappointment, there was no sign of Daniel. Nor did the bedtime fare of warm goat's milk provide a calm sleep. Instead, her nights became more disturbing.

Her dreams were now filled with a cloying black fog in which a menacing presence stalked her, startling her awake, panicked. Reluctant to return to those unnerving visions, she lay awake until exhaustion overcame her. She would have much rather been haunted by the young woman's desperate pleas which had suddenly ceased.

Each morning, she dragged herself out of bed and stumbled through the day, with barely the energy to churn butter, bake bread, wash laundry, or weed the garden. When evening came, she sat on the stoop staring sightlessly into the distance. At bedtime, she collapsed gratefully on her pallet, yet reluctant to give way to sleep, certain that terrifying nightmares awaited her.

On a Saturday morning in mid-May, while the boys were at market with their father, Jenna and her mother did the usual weekend cleaning and cooking in preparation for Sunday, as unnecessary work on the Sabbath was forbidden. Weary from the effort, Jenna was sitting on the front step with her eyes closed, resting her head against the door lintel, her mind wandering to the mountain, the goatherd's wife, and the charming boy from the city.

"Jenna!"

Blinking, she squinted in an effort to see who was calling her name.

"Jenna, it's me."

"Me?"

"Daniel, from the trees. You know, the wood sprite!"

As her vision cleared, there he was, his arms crossed, his face lit with an impish smile.

"Daniel!" He seemed to have materialized out of her thoughts. Maybe he *was* a wood sprite! Or a spirit of some sort. "How did you get here?"

"Walked, of course. It's a lovely morning. I said I would come, didn't I? Sorry that it took me so long. Will had to go back home, and I made the trip to the city with him, but I've come back to spend the rest of the summer on the mountain."

"It's good to see you, Daniel."

He sat down next to her, frowning. "Are you well, Genevieve of the Trees?" he asked in a concerned voice.

Jenna looked away. "I'm fine. Why?"

"You look a bit pale, and you have dark circles under your eyes, like you aren't sleeping."

"I just tire out easy, that's all." She heard the defensiveness in her voice.

When he didn't respond, she turned to see him watching her with questioning eyes.

"What?" she asked, trying not to squirm at his intense look.

Just then, Jenna's mother came around the corner of the house with Peter in tow. "Well, and who is this young man?" she asked.

"I'm Daniel, the son of the cousin of the goatherd, ma'am," he said, jumping up and bowing.

Rachel laughed. "Abram told us all about you, Daniel."

"I've come to visit, as I promised Abram and Jenna."

"Well, Abram and the boys are at market with their father. They'll not be back til late in the day. Would ye care to stay for noon meal, or do jest women for company turn ye a bit?"

He chuckled. "Oh, there's Peter, here. That makes two men and two women, so we're even."

Peter stood proudly at being called a man.

Rachel smiled again. "Well, yes, as ye say. Jenna, fetch me a bucket of water."

"I'll do it," Daniel said. "Let Jenna rest, she looks so peaked."

Jenna sat up taller at her mother's stare.

"Aye," Rachel said, her brow wrinkled, "she's been a bit sallow about the gills."

"Mama, I'm fine. I'll fetch the water." Jenna glared at Daniel. Why did he have to call attention to her this way?

Daniel frowned and narrowed his eyes. Then he suddenly grinned and started dancing a jig. "No, let me. See, I've got energy to spare."

"Silly boy," Peter intoned.

"You're sillier," Daniel said, grabbing Peter's hands and spinning him in a circle.

Peter giggled with delight.

Jenna's annoyance seeped away as she watched Daniel clown with Peter.

Daniel stayed to eat, helping Rachel set the table, entertaining Peter with silly rhymes. After lunch Rachel said, "Jenna, why don't you take young master Dan'l on a walk to your weeping willow."

Jenna sighed. "It's such a long way. Can't we just sit a bit by the oak tree?"

"You'd rather sit than walk to the brook? Why Jenna, that isn't like you."

Daniel shoved her gently with his shoulder. "Come on, Jenna. Bet you can't run faster than a wood sprite."

"You're a wood sprite? Now, I'm a might likely to believe that." Rachel chuckled.

"Don't pay any attention to him, Mama. He's more of an imp than a wood sprite." Jenna smiled back at her mother.

Her mother patted Jenna's hand. "The sunlight'll do ye good. Ye've not been out to the meadow in a long while."

Jenna blinked back unexpected tears at the tenderness in her mother's voice.

"Aye, Mama."

Jenna led Daniel through the woods by their house, across a field, and toward the castle ruins which sat on a small rise. Daniel chattered away about his trip to the city, but his words flowed over her like a rush of water over ground too parched to absorb moisture. She walked in the numbed, mindless state that had marked her recent days. When she reached the willow tree, she sank in weary relief in its refreshing shade.

"Jenna, are you sure you aren't ill?" He plunked down next to her, eyeing her intensely.

Jenna looked back through bleary eyes, frowning at him. *I just want to sleep.*

"Are you still sleeping restlessly the way Abram said? Is it because you have bad dreams?"

Jenna crossed her arms and quickly looked away. She didn't want to think about nightmares in the middle of the day, in the shelter of her tree. She bit her lip to keep it from trembling.

"Jenna," he said softly, "tell me about it."

It was tempting. *He would listen. He wouldn't think I was silly or acting like a baby.*

"I've always had trouble sleeping," she began in a very quiet voice.

"Always?"

"As long as I can remember." She sighed, staring into the stream of water that splashed over and around mossy rocks.

"Mama says it's my imagination and I should put it to sleep with the rest of me at night. But I don't think it's my imagination that conjures up those dreams."

"Jenna," Daniel prodded gently, "Tell me about your nightmares."

Jenna scrambled to her feet, glaring at him. "I didn't say I had nightmares!"

Daniel stood up beside her. "But you do, don't you? You said the word 'conjures.' That's a scary word."

She shivered. "I don't talk about them."

"Ever? To anyone?" Daniel was quietly insistent.

"What good would that do? Who could stop them?" She strode away with rapid steps, then slowed to pick up pebbles along the creek bank, wandering some distance away.

She peered back at Daniel from time to time. He sat tossing sticks into the water and watching them float downstream.

When she had calmed down, Jenna returned to sit beside him. With a slightly trembling breath she said, "You see, it's not just... the dreams. It's that... like a silly little girl... I'm afraid of the... dark."

She hid her face in her hands, ashamed to look her new friend in the eyes.

"Oh, Jenna." She felt a comforting hand on her shoulder. "Everyone is afraid of something. Who isn't a bit afraid of the dark? It's just logical."

She looked up, brushing dampness from her cheeks. "Logical? Really?"

He patted her shoulder. "Of course." His voice was full of confidence, like a teacher instructing his student. "The dark is, well, dark. It hides things. Things that could be dangerous. In the city, they light streetlamps so you can see your way and watch out for thieves. Out here in the country, there could be wild animals roaming in the night."

He made it sound so matter-of-fact, so very reasonable. She leaned back against her willow tree, pondering his explanation, then asked hesitantly, "What about the dark in dreams?"

"Are all your dreams full of dark? Like night?" He continued in his calm, easy voice.

"Lately, well, more like a dark fog."

Daniel reached up, breaking off a willow branch. He stripped its long leaves and began weaving them into shapes, saying nothing.

She pulled up her knees, wrapping her arms tightly around them, rocking slowly. "There's something in that fog," she said, a tremor running through her.

"You can tell me," he encouraged softly, his eyes on his busy hands. "I promise I won't tell anyone."

A tightness grew in her chest as she tried to find the words that would describe her nighttime terror. "I'm in a fog, a dark fog. It's thick. Almost thick enough to touch." Her breath grew shallow as the fear in her dreams began creeping into her body. "I'm walking, and I sense something."

Daniel's hands froze. "Something?" His voice was a barely a whisper.

"I can't describe it. It's a shadow, a shape, and it... " She began to tremble.

Daniel suddenly grabbed her shoulders. "Stop!" he cried. "You don't have to... just... stop there."

After a moment, he took his hands away. "It's okay, Jenna, I didn't mean to startle you. You just, well, you look exhausted. Why don't you lie down a while and rest? I'll sit here and keep you company."

He took off his light outer shirt and folded it. "Here."

Jenna, too tired to refuse, lay her head on the makeshift pillow and very soon lost herself in a dreamless sleep. The sun was much lower in the sky when she awoke.

"Hello, sleepy head," Daniel greeted her as she sat up and stretched. "You look more rested."

"I do feel much better. What have you been doing while I slept?"

Daniel showed her the woven willow branch figures and entertained her with invented lives for each of them. He didn't mention her nightmares again.

By the time they walked back to the cottage, Abram and the others were home from market. Daniel stayed to supper and amused them with animated stories about his family and life on the mountain. To Peter's delight, Daniel gave him the woven willow people.

When he got up to leave, Jenna's mother said, "Ye must come ta visit us again, Young Dan'l.

"Thank you, Mistress, I'll do that."

Jacob suggested Abram hitch up the mare and give Daniel a ride across the valley. Thomas offered to ride along.

As the boys set off, Daniel turned to wave at her. "Bye, Jenna!"

"Bye, Jenna," Abram mocked in a sing-song voice, then gave a surprised "Hey!" as Daniel smacked him on the arm.

"Bye, Daniel!" Jenna waved with a smile.

One morning at breakfast, several days after Daniel's unexpected visit, Jenna's father announced he had received a letter from his Aunt Myra. Their father's aunt wrote several times a year, and Jacob always read a bit of it out loud to them. It was exciting to hear about the goings on of a distant city, more so now that she knew it was Daniel's hometown. She could more easily visualize what Aunt Myra described from all of Daniel's stories.

Aunt Myra always wrote a personal greeting to each of the children, wishing them well in their specific endeavors. When he finished the letter, Jacob looked thoughtfully at them. "She's getting on in years, you see, and wants to see something of my family."

"Is she coming to visit, then?" Abram asked.

"No, some of us are going to visit her."

That unexpected news sent a chill of excitement through Jenna's bones.

"Who?" Thomas was nearly bursting with anticipation. Jenna knew how thrilled he'd be to see the ocean and sailing ships.

"Well, your Ma is not in favor of a long journey for herself or little Peter, and Joshua will need to tend to the tiling."

Jenna saw her oldest brother trying to hide his disappointment.

"Joshua is to be the man of the house and look after his mother and little brother and see that all goes well in my absence. He is a trustworthy young man."

Joshua turned a deep shade of pink. His brothers looked at him with awe at this rare fatherly praise.

Jacob continued, "Since Thomas will have no time for such a trip once he's bound to the cooper, it'd be right that he come along, as well as Abram."

The two brothers grinned at each other.

"Aunt Myra especially asked to see Jenna, as she is our only girl child."

Jenna thought of two small graves in the village churchyard. She barely remembered her sisters who were born after her and were lost to fever when she was six. Every year on the anniversary of their death, the family laid flowers by the tiny headstones.

"When will we be going, Papa?" Jenna asked, hoping she could endure such a long trip.

"We'll go the first Monday of June."

Jenna, wedged in a front corner of the two-wheeled cart, huddled deeper into her woolen cloak. An unusual cold, damp mist hung heavily in the early June morning. To either side of her, the trees of the thick, hardwood forest were black sticks in a white cloud. She watched the rutted road behind her vanish into a wall of fog a mere stone's throw away.

Thomas and Abram, sitting just beyond her reach at the open end of the cart, kicked their long legs for warmth. The heavy air muffled the sound of the mare's hoofs and the turning wheels. Even the birds were eerily silent. Suddenly, a crow's harsh caw echoed from an unseen treetop, splintering the silence. The boys jumped, making Jenna chuckle.

Abram growled at his sister, "That's not funny, Jenna."

"Scaredy cat," Thomas taunted his younger brother.

"It startled you too, Thomas," Jenna interjected.

"You hush back there," their father, Jacob, said sternly over his shoulder from his seat at the front of the cart, and they fell silent again.

An hour later they came to a crossroads anchored by a large tavern. The smell of roasting meat wafted across the air, making Jenna's stomach growl. Her father stopped so they could have their fill of bread and cheese and cider and give the mare a drink from the watering trough. The cold day had driven other travelers into the warmth of the public room, so there was no one to converse with them. They ate their lunch quietly and were on their way again.

By late afternoon, her brothers started bickering the way that weary boys do.

"Stop knocking against me."

"I didn't. It was the cart shifting. Stop smacking me."

"I only smacked you because you knocked against me."

"I didn't do it on purpose."

"Well, then, hold onto the side."

Jenna was surprised that their father, usually quick to squelch any argument between her brothers, let them squabble. Jenna found their voices, regardless of what they said, a comfort in the bleak afternoon.

"Papa, will we get there before dark?" She tried to make her voice light.

"Yes, Jenna, we'll get there before dark." He said it in a voice tender enough to curl up in. Jenna whispered in return, "Thank you, Papa."

After a long afternoon's journey, they stopped for supper only long enough to wolf down the cold meat pie and the second jug of cider. Jenna thought of Mama, Joshua, and her younger brother, eating supper by the fire in the cozy kitchen. They seemed so far away. She wanted to be excited about this journey, like journeys in the stories Papa told them in the long winter evenings and the ones she read out of the storybook that had been her father's in childhood. But some inexplicable sense of dread stirred in her stomach.

She was exhausted when they finally reached a hill overlooking the coast. They were just in time to see a brilliant red-orange sun drop out of the clouds and cast a shimmering light on the blue-green sea and the town sprawling along it.

Jenna scrambled from the back of the cart to stand next to Thomas and Abram. Alert now, she gazed at the wondrous view of the ocean streaked with rays of gold and crimson and the tall-masted sailing ships, anchored in the harbor, bobbing gently on the tide.

"Papa, how long did you live in Westerfordshire?" Jenna asked as she took in the amazing sight of brass weathervanes atop church steeples gleaming like lanterns as they reflected the setting sun.

"Until the time I was fourteen," he replied, a rare smile creasing his face. "When I was young, my mother and I lived with Aunt Myra in the times my father was away to sea and after my... Well, then I stayed with her while I was apprenticed to the tile maker."

"Our grandfather was a sailor?" Thomas' voice echoed Jenna's amazement.

We know so little of our father's family. Her mother's two sisters and their families lived some miles east in the next valley. After harvest, the families gathered for an annual weekend visit. But they had never met any of their father's family.

"Aye, aye," Jacob replied gruffly. "Come on now, let's be going before we are still on the hillside when it gets too dark to see."

As they rode into the town, Jenna was amazed at all the buildings set one against another—houses, churches, shops, taverns—and the cobblestone streets, creating a wonderful clip-clop of hoofs against rock. She wondered how Daniel could be content on the mountain after living in such a thrilling place.

After turning this way and that on streets and lanes in the growing darkness, her father stopped on a quiet street in front of a two-storied, half-timbered house with shutters and a door the color of a robin's egg. Three stone steps led up to the wooden door, adorned with a brass knocker.

"Here 'tis," Jacob said, handing the reins to Thomas as he stepped down from the seat. He stood a moment staring at the house before he squared his shoulders, strode up the steps, and tapped the brass knocker sharply, twice.

The door was opened by a woman in a gray woolen dress with a stained apron and a dust cap struggling to contain gray hair the texture of straw. She eyed them warily, taking in their travel-worn clothes and their time-beaten horse. But then a smile slowly warmed her face. "Why 'tis young Jacob."

"Yes, Livia, it's me, not so young now. We're expected, I believe."

"Aye, ye are. Your aunt's a sittin' by the fire in the parlor and I've been tryin' to keep a meal warm for ye," she said in a voice half full of irritation and half full of welcome.

"You needn't have bothered. We ate on the road."

"Pash. Travelin' always makes a body hungry. And I bet those strappin' lads of yourn wouldn't object to a bit 'o beef."

Abram and Thomas both said, "No, ma'am," at the same time.

Jenna's father nodded in the direction of the horse. "Where should we bed the mare?"

"Take it 'round through the gate to the barn. You know where 'tis," Livia said, as though Jenna's father had been there just last week.

Jacob pointed to the gate in the stone wall which spanned the distance between Aunt Myra's house and the neighbor's home. He instructed Thomas and Abram to take the mare to the barn, unhitch her, rub her down, and give her some hay.

"Wash up at the trough in the yard and come into the kitchen. Jenna, fetch the basket and the bundle out of the cart."

Jenna followed her father as he stepped through the door into a small vestibule. Ahead of them was a hallway and a flight of stairs. To either side were two open doors. Even in the shadowed interior, she could sense a clean well-kept home. The wooden floors shone in the candlelight which cast warm shadows on the white-washed walls. The tangy smell of roasting meat floating down the hallway from the kitchen made her mouth water.

Her father entered the room on the left. Jenna noted the painted wainscoting, a built-in corner desk, and an upholstered divan and chair. An old woman sat in a rocking chair by the fireplace, knitting. Her crisp gray linen dress was accented with a starched white collar and cuffs. Her silvery gray hair was pulled back in a neat bun and adorned with a white lace head covering with two ribbons, untied, that hung down onto her shoulders from the corners.

Though her face was lined with age and care, her eyes were clear and alert. She rose with dignity as they entered the room.

"Jacob."

"Aunt Myra," Jacob replied in a gruff voice, then after a brief pause crossed the room on long strides and swept the old woman up in his arms. Jenna halted in the doorway, amazed to see her quiet, stern father who rarely hugged his own wife in the presence of his children, tenderly embracing this woman Jenna had never met.

When Jacob gently put his aunt back on her feet, she sat down and dabbed a lace-trimmed handkerchief at the corners of her eyes.

"Ah, Young Jacob, you've become quite a man. Your mother would be proud of you." She smiled softly up at him.

Jacob nodded. "Yes, Aunt Myra, I hope as she would be."

He turned and nodded at Jenna, who stepped forward.

"So this is your lovely daughter," Aunt Myra said, eyeing Jenna with a gaze that was soft and loving, yet searching. "She has your mother's dreamy-eyed and will-o'-the-wisp looks."

Jacob remained silent, but Jenna felt his probing stare.

"Her brothers are bedding down the mare and will be in shortly."

"Well," Aunt Myra replied, rising gracefully. "There's time enough for talking later. You must be dropping from hunger and exhaustion." She led the way into the kitchen.

Jacob instructed Jenna to join her brothers and wash up in the yard.

"Livia," Aunt Myra said, "give the girl a cloth. Jenna, you can pull a bucket of water from the well and pour it in the trough. Jacob, you can freshen up in the guest room. Livia just took up some warm water for the wash basin."

Supper was served around a huge oak table in the kitchen which spanned the back of the house. Jenna and her brothers ate silently. The succulent roasted beef, vegetables from the root cellar, fresh bread and sweet butter made a belly-warming late day meal after a bone-rattling journey on the road.

While she ate, Jenna listened as Aunt Myra plied her father with questions. "Tell me about where you live," was the first thing she asked.

Jacob told her about the uplands, where the winters were harsher than those on the coast, but where the springs were soft and the summers green. He told her of the rolling hills and the dark forests and the plentiful game.

She asked about his neighbors, and he told of the hard working country people who paid a heavy burden of taxes to the Lord of the Manor but managed to live quietly and frugally.

She asked if he missed the city, and he told her about the autumn fair and the weekly market and the weddings and baptisms.

Jacob and Aunt Myra talked until Jenna found her head bobbing from exhaustion.

"Oh, me, what kind of a hostess am I? Look at these children, all tired out. Jacob, take the boys out to the stable. They can sleep in the loft as we have nair but two bedrooms."

"We'll put Jenna here by the fire on a feather mattress, as Livia's got her room in the attic."

Jenna's heart constricted at the idea of being alone in the dark in a strange house.

"Nay," Jacob said, "she can sleep in the loft with the boys."

Aunt Myra looked shocked. "But she's a girl! Perhaps we should take the mattress to the attic where Livia..."

"Aunt Myra," Jacob interrupted, "she's used to sharing her sleeping space with her brothers and would probably be lonely here on her own."

Aunt Myra frowned but said nothing. She took a lantern off the mantle, lit it, and handed it to Thomas. "Mind you, blow it out as soon as you're settled." She opened the heavy wooden door that led into the courtyard. More clouds had rolled in, covering the moon and stars, adding to the darkness.

Jenna felt the familiar fear of night creeping into her mind.

"Go on, Jenna," Jacob said. "Abram, show the way."

"There are coverlets at the bottom of the ladder that leads to the loft. Be sure to see that Jenna is warm enough," Aunt Myra said in a motherly way.

As Jenna followed her brothers, she heard Aunt Myra tell her father, "I can't get over how much she resembles your mother."

In the distance, a church bell struck the hour of ten. Though the evening was mild, the darkness seemed so heavy. Jenna hugged her cloak around her, shivering.

Once inside the stable, the boys shut the door. The lantern filled the small space with a soft, yellow light. The mare neighed in her stall, and Abram walked over to pat her gently. Thomas tossed the brightly-colored quilted coverlets into the loft. They made a soft, sighing rustle as they landed on the straw.

Thomas nodded to the ladder. "Go on, Jenna. Abram, give me the lantern. I'll wait until you and Jenna are settled, and then I'll outen it."

Jenna reluctantly climbed into the loft, glancing over her shoulders into the dark corners of the stable where the light didn't reach. She and Abram created three mounded sleeping areas in sweet-smelling straw. Taking off her pinafore, she wrapped her cloak around her day smock and lay on one edge of her coverlet, then pulled the other edge around her. It was a comfortable bed.

After Abram was settled, Thomas blew out the lantern.

The stable was suddenly so dark she could not see her hand in front of her face. Jenna drew in a sudden sharp breath.

"Jenna," Thomas said softly.

"Yes?" Jenna answered, as she emptied her lungs in a long sigh.

"Don't be afraid. If you have—I mean—Abram and I will be right here."

Jenna smiled at her brother's awkward comforting. "All right, Thomas. Goodnight, Abram."

As she drifted off to sleep, she heard Abram say, "Imagine, Thomas, she looks like our grandmother. I wonder why Papa never told us."

She was in a dark place, lit by neither moon nor stars. Cold, black fog surrounded her. She felt her way by putting one foot in front of the other. Someone was calling her name.

"Genevieve. Genevieve Regina."

As she walked in the direction of the voice, the cold intensified, and she sensed something nearby. But in the heavy darkness that clung to her like a thick, invisible web, she couldn't distinguish shape from shadow yet sensed that there was something there.

A shuffling sound behind her stole her breath. Jenna spun on her heels. In the murky gloom, she made out a hooded being, barely distinguishable from the enveloping darkness. Panic crept up her legs, rooting her to the spot.

As the being came near, she could distinguish its outline and heard a rasping breath, a rattling laugh. She sensed it delighted in her fear.

An overwhelming terror swept over her.

Suddenly, someone was screaming.

3

A FAMILY SECRET

Jenna sat in the darkness, clutching her cloak, chilled to the bone. She couldn't stop shaking. Where was she?

"Jenna, Jenna!" Abram's anxious voice reached across to her.

"I'll light the lamp." Thomas' shout echoed around her. She heard him clamoring down the ladder, then suddenly a soft light filled the space. In a moment, Thomas was back, hanging the lamp from a rafter.

He knelt beside her, putting his arm around her shoulders. "Did you have one of your dreams?"

She drew in a sharp breath. One of her dreams? Could Thomas know about her dreams?

It was Abram who answered the question, his voice quietly hesitant. "Sometimes you're restless at night, Jenna. Tossing and turning, even, ah, whimpering a bit, like something in your dream is making you, ah, afraid."

Then he too put his arm around her, so she was held solidly between her brothers.

In the warmth of their embrace, her breath steadied, her shivering slowed. She realized they were in Aunt Myra's barn. When she was finally able to ask, she was almost afraid to hear the answer. "Was that me that screamed?"

Abram's answer was reluctant. "T'was, Jenna, but don't worry, t'was only a dream, aye Thomas?"

"Yes, yes," Thomas said, as though he were trying to assure himself. "Just a dream, lass."

She almost smiled at his attempt to sound more than two years older, then an awful thought occurred to her. "But I—do I always—I mean... wake you like this?"

Abram and Thomas seemed to be deciding something with their glance, but neither replied. She said more forcefully, "Please, tell me, have I woken you before by... screaming?"

Thomas squeezed her shoulders, then standing up, fiddled with the lantern. "Well, no. You've woken us a time or two with your restlessness, but never a'fore with..." He turned and knelt in front of her, taking her hands. "Jenna, what was it that so frightened you?"

Jenna shivered at the thought of that hooded presence, creeping closer.

"It's okay, Jenna," Abram said in nearly a whisper. "Don't think of it anymore. Put it out of your mind."

If only she could.

"Do you think you can sleep now?" Thomas asked, squeezing her hands.

She nodded—though she knew sleep would be a long time in coming—and curled back on her bed of straw.

Abram tucked the coverlet in around her and said in her ear, "Think about the meadow, Jenna, and the wind. And your willow tree."

Jenna's eyes filled with tears, touched at his tenderness. "I will, Abram, I will," she said and closed her eyes.

Jenna woke to the sound of wagon wheels on cobblestones and the creaking of a heavy door. She peered over the edge of the loft just as Thomas and Abram came in carrying a huge pail of steaming water.

Spotting Jenna, Abram said, "You're to have a quick wash up and put on the fresh pinafore that's in your bundle of clothes. Here is a cloth, some soap, and a drying towel from Aunt Myra."

"What? Why should I do that?" She blinked in surprise.

Abram shrugged. "Papa said to hurry because breakfast is near to being on the table. We'll be in the kitchen waitin' for ye." He and Thomas shut the stable door behind them.

Jenna scampered down the ladder. A bath in the morning! And it wasn't even Saturday. She made quick work of washing her face, arms, legs and feet without removing her smock. Tying on her spare pinafore, she vainly attempted to smooth out the creases, then hurried out into the courtyard, past the well, and through the kitchen door.

Once inside, she halted abruptly when all eyes turned to watch her. She became aware her hair was a tangled mess.

Aunt Myra, who sat at the head of the table in the one chair with a back and arms, said, "Come here, child. Let's go get your hair brushed."

Jenna, her face flushed with embarrassment, followed Aunt Myra down the hall and up the steep, wooden steps. They entered a room furnished with a quilt-topped four-poster bed, a washstand, and a chest of drawers, all of cherry wood. The washstand held a flowered china wash bowl, a matching pitcher, and a bone-handled hairbrush. Gray serge dresses and white pinafores hung on wooden pegs attached to a thin strip of wood on the wall near the door. A large wooden chest, secured with straps of leather, sat at the foot of the bed.

The sun streamed in two small, four-paned windows beneath the slanted roofline at the front of the house, casting squares of light on the dark oak floor. Jenna froze when she saw the ocean in the distance, and near its edge, breakers dancing their merry waltz on the sand.

"So, you find the sea a lovely thing?"

"Yesterday was the first I ever saw it," Jenna replied, staring at the mesmerizing sight. Hearing a noise, she turned to see Aunt Myra taking a long bundle from the chest, then lay the cloth-covered parcel on the bed and untie the closures, revealing a starched white apron and blue linen dress.

"Come here, child. I think this'll fit you. You look about the size."

Aunt Myra helped Jenna peel off her wrinkled clothes and put on the dress. Not only was it a lovely deep blue fabric, it was wondrously decorated. The bodice, long sleeves and upper skirt were covered with tiny silver buttons and multi-colored beads sewn in intricate designs and swirling patterns. Embroidered stems and leaves connected beads to create flower shapes.

"It's so lovely," Jenna said tenderly, tracing her fingers gently over the beads.

"T'was your grandmother's. It's really a party dress, but the apron will cover most of the decoration and make it more of a day dress."

Jenna turned around so Aunt Myra could do up the fastenings and tie on the crisp, white bibbed apron. Taking the brush from the washstand, the older woman sat on the edge of the bed and began to carefully untangle Jenna's long, thick, knotted hair.

"I used to brush your grandmother's hair just like this," she said softly. "I was the eldest sister, and she was the baby of the family."

Jenna relaxed into the rhythmic brushing.

"Such beautiful hair she had, like yours, thick and full of life of its own. It never would stay in plaits and ribbons but was always escaping to stray about her face. As for her eyes, they were greener than yours. While yours have lots of green flecks in them, hers could be nearly sea-green. A most unusual color."

Aunt Myra went on in her quiet way, the rhythm of her speech matching the long, gentle strokes of the brush. "She was a beautiful little girl, but a stubborn one. There were two brothers between us. She was spoiled because she was the youngest and had older brothers."

Closing her eyes, Jenna saw her grandmother standing here, having her hair brushed by her older sister. Jenna often wished for an older sister.

"She was especially spoiled after our mother died." Aunt Myra's voice was like a lullaby. "I was seventeen. She was six. She loved the seashore, collecting colorful shells and sea-smoothed stones washed up by the breakers, spending hours digging in the sand or staring at the waves. She watched the ships in their coming and going and spoke of marrying a sailor who would bring her beautiful shells from other seashores."

Jenna saw the little girl running along the seashore, her hair blowing, her cheeks flushed, her eyes dancing like the waves on the sand.

"Her favorite found treasure was a little sea-green bottle that matched the color of her eyes. It had an iridescence, like the sun on the breakers, like it belonged on Neptune's table."

The old woman's story came and went like waves on the beach, like the soft strokes on Jenna's hair. Soothing. Hypnotic.

"She grew up to be beautiful, your grandmother did. She was a coquettish slip of a girl, who had the boys standing on their heads to gain her attention. She strung them along, playing with their hearts like they were tops that she could spin and let go of when she was tired of the game."

Jenna felt bereft at her own lack of graceful beauty.

"The moment she met your Papa's father, she set her cap for him. He was already a captain. His family were shipwrights and sailors with a long history of seafaring."

Jenna visualized the handsome young man in a uniform with brass buttons, like the king's soldiers who occasionally marched through their village.

"He thought her silly and willful and didn't take her seriously. She did outrageous things to get his attention."

Jenna longed to ask about those outrageous things.

"She finally succeeded, though I believe she did most of the wooing. Unbecoming and nearly scandalous. She got the marriage she wanted in the end, but it wasn't a happy one."

Aunt Myra was silent for so long, Jenna thought the story was over. Timidly she asked, "Why wasn't it a happy one, Aunt?"

"Your Grandfather was usually at sea, where he was happiest," the old woman continued, as though she had never stopped talking. "The reunions were painfully joyous and the leavings like a burning iron to your grandmother's soul."

In her mind's eye, Jenna saw the tears on her grandmother's young face, as she watched her beloved captain sail out of the harbor. She felt tears welling in her own eyes.

"After your father, young Jacob, was born, she became as desperate at mothering as she had been at catching her beau's eye. She seemed terrified that something was going to happen to the baby. She sat long hours by the cradle, watchful and wary, as if to ward off some evil spirit that might slip in with the shadows."

Jenna began to feel chilled in spite of the bright sun beaming in the window.

"Some long time later little Joanna was born, and your grandmother seemed to relax. Jacob was at sea soon after the new baby arrived, and your grandmother began to go to dinners and dances, though it wasn't seemly without her husband. She always talked one of our brothers into being her escort, so it was less of a scandal."

There was a tremor of sadness in Aunt Myra's voice.

"When Jacob was at sea, your grandmother came home here to live. She didn't like being in the cottage alone. I tended the children a lot."

A cloud drifted across the sun, throwing the room into unexpected shadow. Jenna felt her chest tightening, anticipating an unwanted turn of the story.

"The night little Joanna took suddenly sick, I was taking care of the children, as your grandmother was at a dance. I sent a servant to fetch the doctor and another one to bring your grandmother home, but she couldn't be found."

Jenna heard the sound of Aunt Myra's arms falling to her side.

"The doctor came and went, saying t'was nothing to be done for the wee one but comfort her. I sat by the fire rocking and rocking her. Your father was seven, upstairs asleep. When your grandmother came in, I asked her where she'd been. She said she'd met an old beau at the dance, and they'd gone for a walk by the sea."

Jenna stood, unmoving, breathless.

Aunt Myra sighed wearily. "She took the baby from my arms, but it was too late. It was then that I saw my lovely young sister had sand in her hair."

Jenna sat next to her, the terrible sadness of loss wrapping itself around her heart. She thought of her own little sisters, lost to fever. Jenna knew instinctively that Aunt Myra had never told this story to anyone, not even Jenna's father.

"She never cried," Aunt Myra said, suddenly interrupting the silence. "She sat a whole day rocking the little thing. Wouldn't give her up. Then she lay on this bed for two weeks, staring at the sea. Didn't even see her little one buried, so stunned with grief she was."

Jenna heard the sound of the sea in the distance and felt Aunt Myra's arm around her shoulders as she began to rock her gently side to side in the rhythm of the never-ceasing sea. Jenna closed her eyes.

"One day it was storming. A dreadful cold chill crept into the house. I came upstairs to see how she was faring, and she was gone! The bed sheet lay flung back..."

Jenna could see the bed behind them, empty and rumpled.

"I knew right away where she had gone. I found her at the edge of the sea, kneeling in the sand by the water's edge in the pouring rain, sobbing. Burying her little bottle, muttering something about it being an offering to the sea. She was delirious. I brought her home and put her to bed; she was burning with fever. And then..."

Jenna felt a dread she could not name.

"Then she cursed her husband, cursed Jacob. 'It's your fault,' she said to Jacob, who was still at sea. 'You are to blame. You always loved the sea more. So go home to your mistress, the sea—let her take you and your ship to her heart.'"

Jenna felt Aunt Myra tremble at the awfulness of her memories.

"She slipped into unconsciousness and never woke up. The day we buried her, we learned Jacob's ship had gone down in a storm, within sight of land, up along the western coast. All hands were lost."

Jeanna barely breathed as the story settled back into memory, the words fading like the sunlight in the ever-cloudier day. A mourning dove cooed in the nearby tree, sighing for a heritage of sorrow sheltered within one house. When Aunt Myra finally began to stir, Jenna opened her eyes and stood, wiping away traces of her tears.

"Aunt Myra," she said softly, "what was my grandmother's name?"

The old woman looked at her oddly.

"Why child, don't you know?" she said, as she began tying back parts of Jenna's hair in ribbons. "It's the same as yours. You were named for your grandmother. Genevieve Regina."

Breakfast was a silent meal.

Aunt Myra was distant and withdrawn, unlike the warm and welcoming hostess of the night before. She seemed to have suddenly aged. Jenna barely touched the fresh-grilled sausage or the warm cornbread, a meal at home that would be a holiday dinner instead of a weekday breakfast.

The boys, after eyeing Jenna's attire with amazement, ate with their usual appetite, but minded their manners and didn't speak unless spoken to. Jacob made no comments.

After breakfast, Jacob told the boys to chop wood, clean the stable, and do any chores Aunt Myra had for them.

"Then you are free to roam. If you go to the seaside, don't you be going in the water, for you haven't been taught to swim. Stay clear of the dock men, as they'll not take kindly to your staring and questioning. Keep together and be mindful. At your age, you could be carried off to sea by a press gang. Be home when the clock tower strikes noon."

Abram and Thomas nodded soberly at their father's grim words.

To Jenna's surprise, her father added, "Once Jenna's helped Livia with the dishes, she will be going with me on an errand. We will be gone the rest of the morning."

While Jenna helped Livia clean up, her father and his aunt sat in the parlor near the fireplace, conversing. As Jenna walked dishes to the corner cupboard, she overheard snatches of their conversation.

"...the dress... upstairs..."

"In the chest. I've had it..."

Without meaning to, Jenna slowed her pace.

"I don't like it, Aunt Myra. She's not used to such fancy clothing."

"Ah, Jacob, I've no use for it, and she's your only daughter."

"Aye, true."

"And it's your mother's dress."

"You said that, but it makes her look different."

Jenna dawdled, slowly stacking the crockery into the cupboard.

"Yes," Aunt Myra said, "she's the spitting image of your mother at that age, just verging on womanhood. Jenna has the same dreamy eyes, the same distant look. Do you remember your mother?"

"No." Jacob's reply was curt and after a short pause he added sternly, "It's time she gives up that dreaminess. She's nearly a young woman."

"Jacob," his aunt responded with a chuckle, "You're from a family of dreamers. You can't help but pass it along. It's in the blood."

"I'm a hardworking man, Aunt Myra. I left the city for the simpler life of the country." The anger in her father's voice took Jenna by surprise.

"I'd wager you can still tell stories. You could always weave a tale by the firelight," Aunt Myra contradicted.

Jacob snorted. "Tales. They get you nowhere. Same as dreams. What did dreams of distant lands get my father... Jenna!"

Jenna started, nearly dropping the plate in her hand. She walked to the doorway, trying to look innocent.

"Aye, Papa?"

"You helping Livia out there?"

"Aye, Papa."

"Good. Now go out and see how your brothers are faring in the barn with their chores and come tell me."

"Aye, Papa." Jenna scurried to the kitchen door, embarrassed at being caught eavesdropping.

The church bell was ringing nine as Jenna climbed into the seat of the cart beside her father. He was wearing dark serge pantaloons with clean stockings, a short waistcoat, and a soft cotton cravat around his neck. Jenna wondered what kind of errand they had with both of them dressed in Sunday finery.

With the fickleness of June on the coast, the sun came out from behind the clouds and the day warmed. Jenna watched the cityscape unroll as her father steered the cart, though her mind was filled with questions about their errand. But she did not speak them aloud, for it was clear her father was in an unapproachable mood.

In the breaks between the houses and shops, she could see the sails of a ship skirting the bay. The tantalizing glimpses filled her head with thoughts of Jacob, Genevieve, and baby Joanna and the sad end to which they came. *I know something about Papa's mother that he does not.*

A family secret.

The streets were busy, and travelers passed them continually, nodding a "good morning," or bidding "good day to ye." If Jenna had not been so lost in her thoughts, she would have been captivated by all the sights and sounds. She barely noticed when they turned down a wider street. Her father pulled the cart up to a hitching post and dismounted.

"Jenna."

Jenna eyed her father questioningly.

"We're here to see someone."

"Aye, Papa?" she asked, her curiosity piqued at the odd tone in her father's voice. They had tied up in front of an elegant brick house surrounded by a black iron fence. Near the gate a sign swayed gently in the spring breeze.

"Doctor James Carmichael," she read out loud. Then, her heart racing, she asked, "Doctor? Are you sick, Papa? Is that why we've come to the city?" Thoughts of her grandmother and baby Joanna rushed into her mind, and she felt suddenly lightheaded.

"No, Jenna, I am quite fine. It's just that your Mama and I, well." He stopped, his face troubled, his words sporadic. "We thought you have trouble sleeping sometimes, you see, and we thought, well, we thought maybe a doctor could help."

Jenna stared at her father, stunned. "You *know* I have trouble sleeping?"

So, it wasn't just Abram and Thomas that knew about her restless nights.

"Aye. You seem to be disturbed by your dreams. And some times... you... wander about in your sleep."

"There was only that one night, Papa, last month. I've never done it before."

"T'was the first time you ever left the house."

Jenna's mind reeled. She woke others with her restless sleep and nightmares and had wandered often about the cottage in her sleep? She remembered none of it.

"That's why... " Jacob's voice trailed off. "Come, now, let's be at this and we'll go afterward and get a sweet cake."

The visit to Westerfordshire wasn't about seeing Aunt Myra, she realized. That was an excuse. *But I'm not sick, am I? I don't have a fever.*

She had never been to a doctor. At home Mama treated whatever fevers or ailments that befell anyone in the family with herb teas or concoctions fetched from Annie on the mountain. She felt a pain in the pit of her stomach as Jacob took her by the arm and walked her hurriedly to the door. He lifted the imposing brass knocker and tapped it firmly. *Rat-a-tat-tat.*

A moment later, a man dressed in a black frock coat, with a waistcoat, tight fitting breeches, and buckle shoes opened the huge wooden door.

"We're here to see the doctor," Jacob said in a forceful voice. The man looked at them haughtily. "We're expected," Jacob added tersely, handing him a note.

With a sniff, the man walked off and left them standing on the doorstep. Jenna saw an angry blush stain her father's cheeks.

The pain in Jenna's stomach intensified. The fancy-dressed servant returned shortly and showed them into a small, unoccupied parlor, then walked through a door to the left of the fireplace.

"This is where we wait," Jacob said, nodding to a spindle-backed chair where Jenna sat down. Her father sat next to her.

From her seat Jenna admired the flowered wallpaper and ornate plastered ceiling. She smiled at the sound of the gold-trimmed clock ticking the minutes loudly on a polished wooden mantle. But in spite of tall windows flanked by boldly patterned drapes, Jenna thought the room cold and austere after the warmth and welcoming of Aunt Myra's house.

The servant came back through the door and said, haughtily, "The doctor will see you now," then walked across the parlor and out another door.

The sound of someone clearing his throat brought Jenna's attention to a tall, thin man, about the age of her father, dressed in a cut-away coat with a brocade vest and a high-necked shirt. He wore breeches similar to the servant's, with stockings and buckled shoes, but more elegant.

He looks like a preacher in fancy clothes. And not a pleasant one either.

Jacob stood, and Jenna did the same.

"So, you're Myra's nephew?" The doctor's demeanor was as stiff as his clothing. To Jacob's "Aye," he said, "Come, we'll talk in here."

Jenna started to follow, but the doctor held up his hand.

"You stay here." His voice was cold.

Jenna remembered her manners. "Yes, sir," she said, curtseying, as her father followed the doctor into his examining room and closed the door behind him.

She returned to the uncomfortable chair, but restless, got up and walked to the fireplace to take a closer look at the painting above it. As she examined the realistic image of horses and hunting dogs, Jenna tried unsuccessfully to ignore the conversation which escaped around the unlatched door.

The doctor was talking. "So, tell me. I've the original letter you wrote. Surprisingly well written, I must say. I didn't expect so much clarity in a..."

"Country man?" Jenna blinked at the tone in her father's voice.

I should go back to the chair and sit down, so I can't overhear them, she thought guiltily, but her legs didn't obey.

"Well, yes," the doctor was continuing, "I forget that you grew up in the city and are an educated man. Your aunt says you choose to live in the countryside."

"Aye, I do. But let's get on with the reason I'm here."

"Yes, yes, don't hurry me. You said in your letter that your daughter, the young girl you've brought with you, has nightmares."

"Yes. She's slept restlessly for many years from the time she was seven or so."

Since I was seven or so! Why has no one ever told me?

"Restless sleep is not the same as nightmares." The doctor's voice was frosty.

"As I said, from the time she was just past her seventh birthday, she began tossing and turning at night. Muttering in her sleep. Sometimes keeping us awake. As she grew older, she started crying out in the night, as if frightened by dreams. Times were that she screamed and sat up in bed. Though her eyes were open, she'd not seem to see us, as if still lost in sleep."

Jenna hid her face in her hands. *They all know. Everyone!*

"Yes, yes, go on," the doctor's impatient voice filtered through Jenna's thoughts.

Jacob continued his explanation. "She grew wary of the dark. She would no longer play outside the house in the evening, not even on the hottest of summer nights. She'd only go as far as the bench beside the kitchen door, where the light of the house would reach her. She used to take her wee sisters to play in the dooryard, evenings after supper chores were done. Tell them stories. Always full of imagination, was she, our Jenna. A dreamer."

"So, I see. Maybe too much of a dreamer."

"What's that, you say?"

"Never mind. What else is there?" The doctor's tone was irritated.

"Well, and she's taking to wandering."

"Wandering?"

"She did it from time to time as a youngster. We'd wake up and hear soft footsteps. We'd jump out of bed, and we'd find her staring at the door, as if waiting for something, or someone. And then…"

"Yes, yes, go on, man."

"As of late her nightmares seem more, hmm, terrifying. It's that, it seems, you see, that she cries out at times as if she has seen the…"

In a fit of sudden wooziness, Jenna sank to the floor, her head spinning.

"Yes, get on with it. I haven't all day here."

Her father said something she could not hear.

"Oh? Really? I see. And have you taken her to see the deacon of your church?"

"The clergyman? No." Her father's voice was alarmed. "I did no such thing. I decided to bring her to you. A doctor."

"Yes, yes. Well, medicine has gotten beyond the superstitions of the church. We left that all behind in the dark days of the past centuries. You made the right decision to seek the answer here."

Although the room tilted around her, she strained her ears to hear. She caught the end of the doctor's question. "… in the day?"

"She helps look after her little brother. Of course, she helps her mother with the cooking and cleaning and the wash. Tends the garden. She's a girl, after all. When she's done with her chores, she likes to walk down by the stream near the old castle ruins."

"She wanders on her own? And sits idle in the middle of the day? Not well disciplined."

"Begging your pardon, sir, I think you are mistaken."

Jenna pictured her father standing taller. "The wife and I teach our children their manners, their prayers, and their proper place in the world. They will do hard but honorable work. They'll be able to make their own way."

"But you've said she's learned to read."

"I was brought up in the city and was taught to read. My sons and daughter need book learning if they're not to be taken advantage of by cunning people."

"But women should keep to their place. They become fretful when someone fills their heads with untoward ideas."

Her father's response was given in a thoughtful tone. "Aye, men and women both have their rightful work. I agree with you. Jenna is a fanciful child, dreamy and sometimes far away in her thoughts, but she knows her place. She is not contrary, just distractible."

Footsteps approaching the unlatched door startled her. She quickly scrambled to her feet and scurried across the room, sitting in the chair just as the door opened.

I'm so wicked, lately. Eavesdropping again.

"Jenna, come here, child. The doctor wants to talk to you."

"Aye, Papa," she muttered, feeling nauseated at all she'd heard.

The doctor stood behind her father. He was watching her with sharp, unfriendly eyes. She looked beyond him into the room which was lined with glass-fronted cabinets. Bottles and jars full of colorful liquids and shiny powders caught her attention. Then she spotted more fearful looking things—knives, prongs, saws, and other implements.

"Sit there," the doctor commanded, pointing to a cushioned bench along the far wall. She crossed the room on trembling legs. The doctor sat on a stool in front of her while her father perched on the edge of a chair next to a desk, leaning forward, his hands resting on his thighs.

She felt like a ragdoll as the doctor's cold hands turned her head to one side and then the other then felt her neck and the shape of her head beneath her hair.

"Now stand and walk across the room."

Quivering, Jenna did as directed. Each time she reached one side of the room the doctor barked, "Again." After a half dozen trips across the polished wooden floor, Jacob protested, "She looks woozy. Can't she sit?"

The doctor made no response. Instead, he told her to sit on the bench and take off her shoes and leggings. Embarrassed, she looked away as he scrutinized her bare feet, ran his hands along her legs, then pushing up the sleeves of her dress, prodded her arms.

"Open your mouth. Now stick out your tongue."

He looks in my mouth as though I were a mare for sale, she thought as the doctor examined her teeth and pushed her tongue to one side and looked at her gums.

The doctor then barraged her father with questions about what she ate, what time she got up, and when she went to bed.

Finally, he was silent, and simply crossed his arms and stared at her with his unblinking eyes.

Jenna tried not to squirm under his intense gaze. She could hear the ticking of the clock in the waiting room and her own breath. She glanced at her father, still seated in the same position, and then looked back at the doctor. Finally, uncomfortable under his silent glare, she looked at her feet, feeling like a prisoner about to hear her sentence.

At last, the doctor ordered, "Put your shoes and stockings back on," and said to her father, "Well, it's clear to me what this is."

The doctor walked to his desk, pulled out the chair, arranged himself carefully on it, took up a quill pen, dipped it in the ink bottle, and began to write in an open ledger.

After a patient, polite silence, Jenna's father asked, "Aye, and then what is it?"

The doctor continued his scribblings as he answered Jacob. "First of all, she's overtired. It's apparent she has not had an adequate night's rest in years. That's the first issue at hand."

"Yes, sire, and what of the cure for that?"

"I'll be giving you a powder that you're to put into warm milk and feed to the girl at bedtime, which is to be promptly at sunset, regardless of the season."

Jenna bristled at his words. *Feed the girl. Does he think I'm a cow?*

"Aye, that we can do."

"The second issue is the weightier of the two."

The doctor looked up from his ledger. He stared over his half-glasses at Jacob.

"I believe she has been given much too much freedom for a girl. She needs to be properly disciplined, given a clear, regular schedule. She needs to be taught to run a household, as will be her station in a few years. If she is disobedient, she needs to be properly punished. Spare the rod and spoil the child, as the Bible says."

Jenna tried to take in the doctor's words. *Too much freedom. Punished.*

The doctor continued in an unfeeling tone. "It's your lack of discipline that has developed a willfulness in her that must be broken. The dreams are a consequence of her lack of moral training and the mistake of teaching her to read. If you insist she learn to read, restrict it to edifying works. *The Bible. Pilgrim's Progress.*"

Jenna felt a deep sadness. *Does Papa think I am spoiled?*

The doctor walked to his glass-fronted cabinet and took out a blue-tinted bottle stoppered with a cork and handed it to her father.

"Start with one pinch in a portion of warm milk each night. Gradually increase that until by midsummer you are using three pinches each night. Use it all up. By the time it's depleted, she should be sleeping well and over these dreams. But remember, it's the discipline that's the most important part of the cure."

"Aye," Jacob responded slowly, then said to Jenna, "Go sit in the parlor while I finish up with the doctor."

Whatever conversation happened, Jenna didn't hear, for the door firmly closed behind her. A few moments later, Jacob came out of the office. The doctor did not accompany him.

"We can be going, Jenna." He took her by the arm and led her out of the house.

They rode away without speaking. She didn't look up until her father said, "I know you wanted to see the ocean." They were on the outskirts of Westerfordshire overlooking a stretch of sand. The sun had once more disappeared behind a gray sky.

Jenna wanted nothing more than to touch the water. "Papa, can I walk by the sea? I want to look for some pretty seashells to take back to Mama and Peter."

Jacob frowned, but said with a sigh, "Very well. For a short time. I'll sit here in the cart and watch ye. But don't get right near the waves. The tides are rough today—a storm out at sea is churning up the waters."

Hopping down, Jenna ran down the grassy slope that separated the beach and the road. A series of small dunes waited to be surmounted. Peeling off her shoes and stockings and holding them in one hand, she ran up the first dune and down the other, breathing in the salt air. As she climbed the last of the dunes, she was met with the roar of the waves.

Everywhere the tumbling, crashing waves lapped at the beach, then clung to it, resisting the pull of the outgoing tide. The gray, overcast sky let loose a sprinkle of misty rain which made a gentle pitter-patter on the sand. All around her, the world was defined in grays, browns, and greens: the gray, swirling sky, the washed-out brown sand, and the grey-green frothing waves.

She felt as though she were standing at the edge of eternity and sensed in the wind and waves the power of some master hand, some powerful creative force. It seemed the waves roared in praise and the sky showered love.

A deep abiding stillness sank into her soul in the way rain sinks into a parched earth. The ocean was a healer, a magician. Walking closer to the water, she saw shells of every size and shape, some broken from the impact of the waves, others unblemished.

She began to gather treasures, giving each lacquered shell, each sand-smoothed stone, each small piece of brown, broken driftwood a careful examination, choosing a choice few to put in her apron pocket. In her search, she came across a small tide pool.

Looking into the shallow waters, she saw her reflection. The beaded flowers and silver buttons on the dress reflected like tiny stars in a murky sky. Momentarily disoriented, she thought she could dive into a different world. Then beyond the reflection she saw a glistening object protruding from the sand.

Reaching in, sending her face into ripples, she tugged at it, but it was well imbedded. She put down her shoes and stockings, rolled up her sleeves, and dug in the tide pool until she triumphantly pulled out a small, rounded bottle with a short neck and a small lip. It was a bewitching shade of iridescent green-blue, like the color of the sea seen from her aunt's window that morning. It fit perfectly into her cupped hand.

"Jenna, Jenna!" Her father called from the top of the dunes. "Come now, 'tis time to be going back."

Jenna wrapped the small bottle in the handkerchief her great aunt had given her and tucked it in the other pocket of her apron.

When she laid her seashells on the table, Jenna was the only one who saw the shock on Aunt Myra's face. She was the only one who heard her aunt say in a stricken voice, "Genevieve Regina, you've got sand in your hair."

4

WOMANLY DUTIES

Their remaining visit was full of adventure.

After a hearty noontime meal, Jacob took Jenna and her brothers for a stroll along the High Street to peer into shop windows and stop for treats. They called in at the shop owned by Daniel's father, where Jacob introduced himself and the youngsters.

Daniel's father was a cheerful man with a hearty laugh and a welcoming smile. He said Daniel had told them all about Jenna and her family. They had a pleasant conversation and as they were leaving, Daniel's father said to Jenna, "You tell young Daniel to mind his manners and his studies up there on the mountain," as if Jenna had any control of the impish boy.

She nodded in agreement, too shy to speak, but soaked up impressions of the shop, the city, and Daniel's father to share with Daniel when she next saw him.

At supper, Aunt Myra tried to convince Jacob to stay a day or two longer, but he gently explained it would not be fair to his wife and oldest son to leave the farm for long.

As Jenna was helping to clear the breakfast dishes the next morning, Aunt Myra handed her a bundle tied in brown cloth.

"As it fits you perfectly, and it was your grandmother's, take it with you, child."

She gave Aunt Myra a tender kiss on her wrinkled cheek. "Thank you, Aunt Myra. I'll be especially careful with it."

It was nearly nightfall when they reached home. The sweet treats and Jenna's treasures were met with cries of delight.

Late that night, Jenna lay wide awake on her straw mattress, her mind swirling with all she had seen and done in the last three days. She could hear her parents talking softly by the hearth. Assured by the soft snoring of her brothers that they were asleep, she crept closer to the edge of the loft.

I'm sure to be punished for this evil habit, she chided herself, but she was certain her father was telling her mother about the visit to the doctor.

"How could such a little thing so content with simple pleasures be so full of terror and haunted dreams?" Jacob was saying. "Abram and Thomas said she had a nightmare the first night we were at Aunt Myra's, though not the second. She seems to be getting worse."

Jenna felt a surge of anger at her brothers for telling tales but brushed it away to concentrate on her parents' quiet words. Her mother said something Jenna could not hear.

"He was an arrogant, self-important, vicious man." Her father's low voice was filled with loathing. "I have no intention of locking Jenna up or giving her a sleeping draught."

Another unintelligible reply from her mother. Jenna could make out her father's frown as the firelight lit his face.

"The one in the lee side?" He seemed to be repeating what her mother had said. Then he paused. "You don't mean, the old woman who..." Jenna saw her father make the sign to ward off evil. "You wouldn't! They say her mother was a witch."

Rachel's answer was clear this time. "Jacob, I didn't think you believed in witches and such."

"Aye, I am a might bit more educated than the country folk around here, but there's things one shouldn't be delving into, and sorcery is one of them. Perhaps she's just a strange woman, alone with no kin. But I've heard enough talk to stay clear of her. I do agree, though, that it's time we gave over more of the keeping of the house to Jenna. She just turned her thirteenth, and we've been too lenient with her, ever since the little ones..."

Jenna crawled back silently to her straw pallet, covering up with her cloak. She'd been chilled the whole journey home and had taken her cloak to bed for extra warmth. Overwhelmed by fatigue, she soon was asleep.

She was standing in a shadowed place. What had brought her here?

"Genevieve. Genevieve Regina. Come. I need you. Please."

Yes, the pleading, desperate voice had brought her here again, always that voice.

A movement caught her eye. Staring into the dark, swirling mist, she watched a shape take form, as though the darkness were congealing into a being. A being that began to drift her way, a being cloacked in a hooded cape of deepest ebony, barely distinguishable from the color of midnight that filled her dream.

A being that exhaled a deep, rattling breath that seemed to come from some abyss within its shrouded form. A being that seemed to ooze hatred.

An icy, clawing fear grasped her ankles, rooting her to the spot. The coldness crept up her body, paralyzing her limbs. As the form came within reach, terror climbed into her lungs, stealing away the air. Sick with fear, she tried to scream, but no scream would come. The being had grasped her neck with skeletal hands.

As bony fingers clenched her throat, shutting off her breath, Jenna felt herself grow limp, her mind filling with the blackness of the night around her.

A burning sensation in Jenna's nose jerked her awake. She sat up, coughing, blinking away tears, rubbing her face vigorously to chase away the stinging. Someone handed her a warm cloth that she pressed against her eyes and nose.

"Is Jenna awake now?" She heard Peter's voice from below the loft.

"Yes, yes." Her mother's voice next to her startled Jenna, and she pulled the soothing towel away from her face.

"Mama? What's wrong? What's happening?" Her words were raspy and her neck tender, as if something had been wrapped tightly around it.

Jenna realized she was sitting on her pallet, oddly drenched in a soaking sweat, her hair plastered to her face. Yet she was shaking from cold, as if she'd emerged from an icy creek. Light poured in the open window behind her, along with a breeze which raised goosebumps on her arms.

"Jacob," Rachel commanded from her kneeling position next to Jenna, "Close the window."

Her father was in the loft? She looked around in confusion. With sudden terrifying clarity, the dream returned, and she flung her arms around her mother, hiding her eyes against her mother's shoulder.

"What is it Jenna, child?" Her mother held Jenna close, rubbing her back. "Come, come. Let's get you down the ladder."

Jenna's legs trembled as she hesitantly descended, her foot guided to each lower rung by her mother's firm hands. Rachel led her into the parents' sleeping alcove and closed the curtain, then gave her a bowl bath and changed her into a fresh nightshirt.

"Lay here, Jenna. I'll get you some broth."

"My neck hurts, Mama." Jenna could hardly swallow.

"Ye must a been tossin' and turnin' in the night and got your cloak all tangled about ye, so as it was near ta chokin' ye." Her mother's usually firm, strong voice quavered.

"Oh," Jenna replied, relieved for the logical explanation. She spent the day prostrate on her parents' rope bed, too exhausted to speak, too listless to move. The family came and went in whispers. That evening, as her mother readied Peter for bed, Jenna asked tentatively, "Mama, can I sleep by the fire?"

"Are ye cold upstairs?"

"It's lighter down here," she replied, unwilling to speak of what appeared in the dark, in her dreams.

"Onst we bank the fire, tisn't much lighter than the loft. Up thair the moon will light the window for ye," her mother replied, patiently.

Jenna found no comfort in the moon staring in at her. She struggled for a reason without giving any details. Hesitantly she said, "Maybe if I sleep downstairs, it won't..." She spoke so quietly her mother had to lean in to hear.

"It won't what?"

Jenna struggled to get out the words. "...maybe it won't... look... for me."

Her mother replied, her voice wary. "Ye dreamt of an *it*?"

"Please, Mama? Please?"

Jenna could not read her mother's face, but was relieved when she said, "Well, then, aye, if it'd be an aid ta ye sleeping."

No one said a word when Rachel settled Jenna by the fire on her straw-filled pallet. She was nearly asleep when her parents came in the door from the stoop.

"I believe ye be right," Rachel was saying in a quiet voice. "The sleeping potion might be jest the thing to let her rest. Then mayhaps she'd nay have those dreams."

In a moment or two, Rachel touched her on the shoulder. "Jenna, sit up child, I have something to help ye sleep."

Jenna sat up, heavy-lidded and weak. She took the tankard from her mother and slowly drank the warm milk. She knew it had the sleeping powder, but she didn't care. If it kept that foul shrouded being away from her dreams, she would eat it by the spoonsful.

It wasn't long until she felt slightly dizzy and deliciously sleepy.

"Goodnight, sweet Jenna," she heard her father say.

Thus, the nightly ritual began.

Over the next weeks, Jenna sat outside on the wooden bench and practiced the despised needlework, trying to make neat hems in handkerchiefs and patching worn frocks and leggings. To her current chores were added milking the cow, kneading and baking the bread, sweeping the cottage, and helping prepare meals.

Instead of listening to the caw of the crow or the coo of the dove in the meadow, she now listened to her brothers squabble over whose turn it was to chop wood, slop the pigs, or take the vegetables to market. Since Thomas had to walk into the village every day to work at the cooper's shop, he said all those chores should be Abram's.

Jenna no longer got her frock dirty or her hair tangled. She didn't come in from a day's romp in the nearby woods with her face aglow. It was too much effort to think about the willow tree or the castle ruins.

"Story, story," Peter would say, pulling at her frock.

"Not now, Peter-eater, I'm busy," she replied.

As the days wore on, she found it harder to wake in the morning, stumbling down from the loft and trudging through the day silent and dragging. Every night she fell into bed with a weary sigh, but had no dreams, neither pleasant nor frightening, and for this she was grateful.

Once in a while, when no one was in the cottage, she would sneak into the chest tucked under the eaves and look at the lovely, beaded dress Aunt Myra had sent with her. Jenna would finger the fabric of the dress and feel a twinge of longing to know more about her grandmother. She felt a bond across time, linked by a common name. Rachel said it was befitting a princess and could imagine no occasion for Jenna to wear it.

Late one Saturday afternoon in mid-June, Jenna was sitting on the stoop with her eyes closed after an exhausting morning of baking, cleaning, and cooking.

"Dan'l! Dan'l!" she heard Peter proclaim and looked up to see her mountain friend swinging her little brother around in circles.

"Hello, Jenna," Daniel said.

"It's good to see you, Daniel." She sat up, feeling lighthearted for the first time in weeks.

He sat down beside her, ignoring Peter, who pestered, "Again, again!"

"In a bit, Peter," Daniel replied. "Go find us two long sticks we can play swords with."

Peter rushed off to do as commanded.

"I got a letter from my father. He said you and your father and your brothers came to visit the store. That was very kind of you."

Jenna nodded. "He was very nice. Not at all like a stranger."

"But you aren't strangers!" Daniel exclaimed. "He knows all about you and your family."

"Yes, he said you told them about us," Jenna replied in a quiet voice, suddenly shy at the thought of being a topic of conversation.

Daniel sat silently for a few moments, then asked, "Did you see a doctor in the capital?"

"Who told you?" Jenna frowned.

"I saw Abram at market, and he told me all about your trip. About visiting the wharfs when you and your father went on an errand. That your father came home with some powder you were to drink in warm milk every night."

Jenna wanted to strangle her blabber-mouthed brother.

"What did the doctor say?" Daniel probed gently.

Jenna's cheeks burned at the memory of the doctor's words.

"I'd rather not." She felt her eyes stinging with tears.

"Whatever it is, it's not like it's your fault."

"But, but..." Jenna held onto her tears and said in a strangled voice, "The doctor said my restless sleep was due to, well, not being properly disciplined."

"What!" Daniel looked as offended as he sounded.

Jenna drew in a ragged breath. "He said I was spoiled. That I was not to roam free, go running in the fields, but to sit proper and learn to be a woman. He said I was willful—that I needed to be obedient and submissive, or I would..."

"You would what?"

"Come to a bad end." Jenna shuddered, thinking of her grandmother as a young woman, losing her baby and cursing her husband. *Could that be my fate?* It was the first time such an idea had occurred to her.

Daniel jumped up, his hands on his hips. "I don't know what that means, but I think the doctor was wrong! To keep you locked up in the house..."

"I'm not locked up in the house, Daniel."

"But not to visit your willow tree or to roam in the meadow. The first time I saw you, you were running in the field, and I thought..."

Jenna stared up at him. "You thought..."

To her great surprise, he turned a shade of red. "I thought you looked like a fairy."

Jenna giggled. "Daniel, you have an imagination as big as the sky."

"Why, thank you." He extended a hand to her. "Enough of all that doctor talk. Come, I've an invitation. Is your mother about?"

"An invitation? For who?"

"Why for you, Miss-Want-To-Know-Everything. Come, help me find your mother."

"She needs no finding. She's in the kitchen."

Just then Peter rushed back, carrying two long sticks. "Play, Dan'l, play!"

"Oh, I see I have a swordfight to attend to first," he said and gave his attention to Peter for a few minutes, then swooped him upside down and said, "Give up now?"

"No! No!" Peter laughed with delight.

"Well, I do. You've won. Now I must talk to your mama, Peter." He put Peter on his feet and walked into the house.

"Wait, wait," Jenna shouted, and scurried after him. When she caught up to him, he already had her mother laughing.

"Slow down, slow down, lad," Rachel was saying. She sat at the table, snapping beans. "Your words are tumbling one o'er the 'nother. Ye've come to fetch Jenna?"

"Yes," Daniel said.

He sat down across from Rachel and began to snap beans as he talked.

"Annie asked that Jenna come stay a week or so. She said since she hadn't a daughter to teach 'bout using teas and herbs for the curin' and why don't Jenna come and stay a wee bit and do some of that learnin'."

He caught his breath as they laughed at his accurate imitation of Annie's accent. "It'll be great fun, Jenna. She said that since I still need some doctoring, you can practice using some of the teas on me. I even volunteered to drink a poultice."

"Ye don't drink poultices—" Rachel began to correct Daniel, but Jenna interrupted.

"Oh, Mama, it's no use. Daniel's head is so full of ideas he wouldn't know a poultice from a poultry."

"Oh, ho! Aren't you the clever one with words." Daniel grinned at her.

Jenna shook her head. "Daniel, I can't go up to the mountain."

"Why not?" Rachel asked.

Jenna gaped at her mother. "Mama, what did you say?"

"I said why not? I think it's a proper idea. Every woman needs to know about tending her sick family, and learning some of Annie's special cures would be fitting. I remember when ye all came down with that fever."

Jenna saw sorrow flit across her mother's face.

"Yes, yes," Daniel chimed in. "It's a right delightful idea. When you aren't learning how to brew these magic cures, I can be telling you my latest story."

"When am I supposed to come to visit?"

"Why as soon as your parents say you may come. Today would be just perfect."

"Today?" Jenna's head swam. "I don't know... I..."

Just then Jenna's father came in the door. "I see we have the young city lad visiting again."

"Good day to you, sir. I've come to steal your daughter."

Jenna was amazed to see her father laugh and slap his knee. "Well, lad, she's a bit young for that. We'd have to pay her ransom in oats and rye. Or is it a bride price?"

"Papa!" Jenna blushed a deep crimson.

Daniel looked taken aback, but then replied in a serious voice, "I'm not well established in the world yet, sir, but come several years in the future, I'd give that some consideration."

"Daniel!" Jenna protested, mortified. She looked at her mother with pleading eyes.

Rachel looked at Daniel speculatively, then smiled at Jenna in sympathy. "Jacob, young Daniel here has come with an invitation fer Jenna to spend some time up the mountain with Annie and learn some of the curing' arts... teas, herbs, poultices, and the like."

Jacob looked at Jenna intensely and then at Daniel. "And what's your job to be in all this education?" he asked in a chiding voice.

"Oh, I'll make up stories to keep her entertained."

"Ah. Well, between your stories and Annie's love of the gab, Jenna's bound to have her ears worn out." He rubbed his face with his large, rough hands. "Aye, it's a good plan."

To Jenna's astonishment, her parents made arrangements in a matter of minutes. Rachel put some clothes in a satchel, and Jacob instructed Abram to give Jenna and Daniel a ride up the mountain.

"If there's anything else you want to take, put it in this satchel," Rachel said to Jenna.

Jenna thought of her grandmother's dress and the sea-green bottle. *What possible use could I have for a fancy dress and a decorative bottle at Annie's house?*

"My cloak, if the night gets chilly," she said.

"Run along and get it."

Jenna scurried to the loft and retrieved her cloak and then the iridescent bottle from the small box where she kept her special things. After some hesitation, she took the dress from the chest in her parents' sleeping alcove and squeezed it into the satchel along with the apron and bottle.

Rachel gave Jenna the sleeping powder and directed her to explain the dosage to Annie. In a time so brief it had her head spinning, Jenna was in the cart with Abram and Daniel, headed to the mountain.

Abram was pleased to be able to spend more time talking to Daniel about Westerfordshire, which he did the entire hour. Jenna sat in the cart, her knees drawn up, her head against the wooden railings, smiling at being out of the cottage.

Annie was all grins and warm greetings. Jenna's initial awkwardness vanished at Annie's straightforwardness. Abram stayed for a supper of stew that had cooked all day over the fire, then took his leave. He surprised Jenna by giving her a kiss on the cheek.

"I'll expect you to come home and cure Joshua of what ails him," he said, laughing. They all knew that what ailed Joshua was the blacksmith's daughter who made cow eyes at him every time she saw him at market.

Jenna laughed too. "I don't know if there's a tea for that ailment."

"Don't forget to take your medicine," Abram called over his shoulder as he mounted the cart. "Mama said to remind you."

After waving goodbye, Jenna dutifully explained her nighttime routine to Annie, who listened carefully then stored the container with the crockery. Jenna helped clean up after supper, then sat with Annie and Daniel on the porch and watched the sun set.

At bedtime, Annie showed Jenna her sleeping alcove tucked to one side of the huge fireplace. It had a narrow rope bed and a thick coverlet. A thin blanket curtained off the area for privacy. Daniel slept in the loft and Annie beneath it. Ezra and Naaman were still up on the high meadow.

"Now into bed, missy. We've a lot of learnin' for ye to be doin' in the next days," Annie said, "so get a good rest."

Jenna climbed into the bed and smiled when Annie tucked the blanket up to her chin. She felt a sense of deep contentment. "Even in summer it's a bit chill in these hills. I've banked the fire but the heat from the chimney will keep you right cozy. If ye get too warm, just open up these curtains here and toss back the comforter."

"Yes, ma'am."

"I've never been blessed with a daughter. We only had the one young un. It feels right nice to be havin' ye about for womanly company. Hope ye find our place to your likin'."

"Oh, yes, yes." Jenna smiled shyly at the goatherd's wife. She felt secure and at ease and looked forward to learning all Annie had to teach her in the days to come.

"Well, then. The angels watch o'er ye, lass."

"Goodnight, mistress Annie."

"Goodnight, missy."

As Jenna drifted off, she remembered the sleeping draught but was too tired to get up and find it. To her amazement she slept well and felt unusually rested in the morning.

The days quickly fell into a routine, with mornings devoted to household chores and afternoons spent on walks in the garden and woods, where Annie pointed out which plants eased a fever and which to use for stomach pain and others that help with the toothache.

"We start out real simple, mind ye, teas made from plants that are easy to spot. Such as chamomile, mint, and garlic from amongst the herbs, and feverfew and witch hazel in the woods. Takes many a year ta larn what part o' which plants are medicinal, be they the roots or leaves or stems," Annie explained.

"Some teas which are pleasant for the drinking are also good for the body and soul," Annie continued, "while others are too bitter for pleasure and best for healin' uses. Then there's some that's poison, the roots bein' good medicine, but then the leaves bein' a danger, maybe even deadly. So's it's best to start easy like."

Jenna learned to recognize plants by their shape, smell, and taste. Each day under Annie's tutelage, Jenna brewed a small portion of tea from different herbs or plants. Then in the evenings after supper she and Annie sat outside churning butter or pounding dried herbs while Daniel regaled them with his tales of faraway places.

"You're as full of fancy as Abram who wants to be a soldier," Jenna said with a laugh.

Each night, Annie tucked Jenna into bed, rested her hand on Jenna's head, and intoned softly, "The angels and the saints be with ye." And each night, Jenna fell into a deep, undisturbed sleep. Not once did anyone call her name in the night, nor did she dream of the dark, hooded presence. Not once did Annie suggest the sleeping powder.

By the end of the week, Jenna's head was whirling with all she was trying to remember. "Annie, you must know more about herbs and plants and healing than anyone in the world."

"Nay, t'isn't so."

"Not so? Who could know more than you?"

"Olmigira."

"Who?" Jenna questioned.

Annie's face was solemn as she said, "The old woman that lives under the mountain on the other side. She knows everything there is to ken about healin'."

"Olmigira," said Jenna. "What a funny name."

"No one knows where she came from," Daniel said with a wink at Jenna. "Everyone says she's as old as the hills themselves."

"Master Daniel, mind ye manners. Olmigira be blessed with a knowledge of the healin' arts. Don't be laughing at what ye don't understand. Ye might be needing her someday."

Daniel looked suitably abased at Annie's mild scolding, and Jenna chuckled.

The next morning, Annie asked Daniel and Jenna to take some things to Ezra and Naaman up on the mountain.

"They're up yonder now in the high mountain meadow on the other side of the ridge and will take ye 'til noon ta walk there. Then I want ye to go down the mountain and see Olmigira. I'm needing several of her medicinal powders."

"'Tis another half day down the mountain," Annie continued. "She lives back o' the woods—in a cave."

"In a cave!" Jenna exclaimed.

"Aye. 'Tis a cozy place. Ye'll see, but ye may have to wait a bit if she's out about gathering her herbs and such. As it'll be late 'til ye get there, she'll invite ye to spend the night by her fire, for she won't want to see two young 'uns out in the woods at night. Specially this night."

Jenna frowned. "Especially tonight? What do you mean, Annie?"

"Why child, with all I've been teaching ye about the proper medicines, I've neglected to teach ye about the phases of the moon and sun. What an addlepated head I have."

Jeanna protested. "I know about the phases of the moon and sun."

"Ha! You know the sun comes up in the east and sets in the west, do ye?" She snorted.

"Of course, I do. And that as the seasons progress toward summer, the sun moves along the horizon north and as the seasons come around to fall, the sun moves back again southward."

"Good, good. And what of the moon."

"Well, the moon runs her cycles. Full moon, waning moon, new moon, waxing moon and full moon again."

"And do ye know what phase of the moon to be finding the healin' toadstools and when to be planting your seed potatoes and what time of the summer to be drying the herbs?"

Jenna stared at Annie blankly.

"And do ye know that midsummer be a magic night and lest ye want to be caught up in magic, ye best not be about in the woods that night?"

Jenna shivered. "The spirits roam on midsummer night."

"Aye. And those that practice the old ways go deep into the woods and dance about a fire and praise the spirits of the earth, wind, sky, and water.

"Witches," Daniel whispered in a laughing tone.

"Master Daniel, those city ways'll get ye in trouble someday. I told ye before about mocking what ye don't understand."

Daniel dropped his head. "Sorry. I was just having fun."

Annie's sigh rattled her whole body. "Do ye think ye're up to the errand?" she asked, looking intently at Jenna and ignoring Daniel.

The idea of walking around in the woods at dusk on midsummer's eve was unnerving. Just being in the woods at night was a thought she could barely embrace. But Annie had been so kind.

"Yes, Annie, I can do it. I'm feeling much less weary than I did when I first came. I think it would be fun to climb up and see Ezra and Naaman and the goats again. And I'll have Daniel for company."

"Sir Daniel at your service, ma'am," he said with a bow.

Jenna laughed. "But where's your trusty steed?"

"I'll have to be my own steed today."

Annie sent Jenna and Daniel to make bedrolls of their blankets. Jenna followed some niggling voice telling her to wrap the beaded dress and sea-green bottle in her bedroll.

Daniel tied them with twine which he used to create shoulder straps for easier carrying.

After Daniel hoisted a satchel full of parcels for the goatherds on his back, Jenna and Daniel set off with their bedrolls hanging from their shoulders and a walking stick in their hands.

On the way, Daniel entertained Jenna with more stories of his adventures in the city and on the mountain and the time passed quickly. With five nights of good rest, Jenna found the trip easier than the last time. The sun had reached its zenith when they got to the crest of the mountain, where they paused briefly, remarking on the gradual slopes that fell into valleys on either side.

An hour later, they reached the goatherd's summer meadow. Ezra and Naaman were pleased for company and delighted at the seed cakes, rolls, cheeses, and vegetables Annie had sent. After a long, leisurely visit, Jenna and Daniel headed back along the ridge.

"Daniel," Jenna said as they walked along, "how do you know where this Olmigira lives?"

"As I said before, all I had to do this spring was wander about. I did a lot of walking and spent a few nights in the woods, sometimes with Will, and sometimes alone. I found a path down the mountain and along a stream through the woods. Near the end of the path there was a shrine to St. Francis with a carving of the saint on the pole and little bells that make tiny chiming noises in the breeze. When Annie told me what to look for, I knew already where to go."

"Is she a holy woman, that she lives in a cave and has a shrine to St. Francis?"

"I don't know," Daniel replied. "I just know she's a healer."

The walk down the mountain took a different kind of energy. Concentrating on their footing precluded much conversation, other than when they stopped to nibble on bread and cheese.

It was early evening when they reached the foot of the mountain and found the path toward Olmigira's cave. A wind was stirring the trees. Jenna shivered to think of being alone in the woods on midsummer's eve.

The charming sound of tinkling bells indicated they were close to Olmigira's cave. As they rounded a bend, Jenna saw the shrine to St. Francis.

Hello, St. Francis. Your woods are lovely, she whispered in her head as they passed by. Before long they spotted an opening on the side of the mountain lit by a dim glow. Jenna wasn't sure if she were relieved or nervous.

Uncertain, she looked at Daniel, who nodded encouragingly. He walked to the entrance and called, "Hello. Hello. We've come from Annie the goatherd's wife for some powders. She sent some cheeses for the price."

The wind was the only reply.

After some moments of silence, Daniel said, "Maybe she's out gathering herbs."

Jenna replied, "Or maybe she's deaf," then gasped as an old, crackling voice behind them said, "Ye called?"

5

OLMIGIRA AND THE WINTER CHILD

The old woman who had appeared as silently as a sigh was as knotted and bent as the walking stick she gripped in her left hand.

Maybe she materialized out of thin air, Jenna thought with a shiver, eyeing what could be an apparition. Olmigira's thin, gray hair lay listlessly on her woven green wool shawl. The frayed hem of her faded brown cotton dress just touched her ankles, showing thick stockings and scuffed shoes. In her right hand, she carried a basket filled with plants and fruits.

She stared at Jenna and Daniel with intense eyes as black as coal.

"Who be deaf, now? I sayed, did ye call?" Olmigira's voice was as shriveled as she was.

Daniel made a courtly bow. "I'm Daniel, a relation of Annie, the goatherd's wife who sent us to fetch your medicinal powders. She sent cheeses as payment. And this is Jenna, daughter of the tile maker in the valley north of the mountain."

"Umm." Olmigira grunted. "Ye are from the city, I see." With what seemed to be a chuckling noise, she shuffled by them and into the cave.

Daniel looked warily at Jenna, who shrugged and followed the old woman through a narrow opening. As they rounded a boulder, the cave opened up into a soaring chamber. Jenna took in the unexpected space with amazed eyes.

Directly across from the opening, a fire burned merrily on a well-made stone hearth, built into the wall above a natural opening in the oval cave. Candles of all shapes and sizes glowed with a soft, flickering light in many of the cave's lower nooks and crannies. Higher on the rock walls colorful tapestries attached by iron pegs provided warmth and beauty.

To the right of the fireplace, a sturdy oak rocking chair beckoned a weary walker. Beside it a well-made patchwork quilt in burgundies and blues lay folded on the straw stuffed mattress of a rope bed.

To the left of the fireplace, a work area was equipped with a long, smooth worktable, a three-tiered shelf, and an herb drying rack. Neatly organized mortars, pestles, and knives lined the back of the worktable; cooking utensils, bottles, clay pots, and baskets filled the shelves; plants of every shape and color hung in various states of dehydration on the rack.

A round rough-hewn table surrounded by three curved benches sat a few steps from the fireplace. Jenna noticed it was laid for three with crockery plates, mugs, and a pitcher. A glazed ceramic vase filled with purple and white phlox rested on a lace table runner in the center.

As if in reply to their unanswered question, Olmigira said with a sweeping gesture, "Sometimes those that ha' received a healin' bring a wee gift," then added, "Put your belongings by the bed and wash up in the bucket by the hearth. I've been waitin' for ye."

Jenna whispered to Daniel, "Did you tell her we were coming?"

Daniel muttered in reply, "Not me. Maybe Annie let her know somehow."

After they did as instructed, Daniel retrieved a wrapped package from his backpack, handing it to Olmigira. She opened it slowly and carefully as if it were a holiday present. She took out the rounds of hard cheese, pressed balls of softer cheese, and loafs of freshly baked bread, smelling each with a deep, inhaling breath, and a long exhaled, "Uhm."

Nodding at them to sit, she used a large, dangerous-looking knife to slice pieces of cheese and bread which she placed on the plates. She then poured a golden-hued liquid into the earthenware cups from the crockery pitcher, after which she stared at them intently.

Daniel crossed and uncrossed his arms under her gaze, while Jenna held her breath and tried not to blink. To Jenna's amazement, Olmigira smiled. It was a smile with few teeth, but clearly conveyed her pleasure.

When their plates were empty, Olmigira passed around baskets filled with sweet, dried berries and crunchy nuts. She put a handful of dried leaves in a crockery teapot and added water from a spouted iron kettle sitting on a trivet in a corner of the fireplace.

"Girl," she commanded Jenna, "wash up the dishes in the bucket there, and you, boy, put another log on the fire."

For living alone, she's used to ordering people around, Jenna thought, but did her assigned chore quickly and efficiently.

When they were finished, Olmigira poured them mugs of tea and motioned for them to sit on the floor in front of the rocking chair. She took a long-stemmed, curved pipe from the mantle, lit it with a long stick she stuck in the fire, and eased herself into the rocker. Drawing a deep puff, she gazed at them with her inscrutable eyes.

"Well, then. Why're ye here?"

Daniel seemed discomfited under Olmigira's unblinking regard. "As I said earlier, Annie sent us to fetch the powders she's wanting. She said you would know which ones."

"Again, I ask ye, why're ye here?" She took a puff on her pipe and let out a long stream of white smoke filled with an odd mustiness that drifted in whirling shapes about the room.

Puzzled at Olmigira's words, Jenna watched as Daniel, looking away, replied in a hesitant voice, "Well, then, ah, yes, there's the powders, but there is another thing."

Jenna grew suddenly wary.

"Ah, well, you see, Jenna doesn't know."

"What don't I know, Daniel?" Jenna said, her voice rising in alarm.

"Aye? She doesn't, does she?" Olmigira's words drew Jenna's attention as the old woman began to rock in a gentle, measured rhythm, her pipe continuing to emit its dancing, almost hypnotizing clouds.

Almost imperceptibly, Jenna found herself moving in time with Olmigira's slow rocking, gripping her mug of tea. In the long silence, her eyelids grew weighted, and her thoughts grew heavy. Wasn't there a question Daniel hadn't answered?

Struggling to stay awake, Jenna touched Daniel on the arm. When he looked her way, she asked in slowly enunciated words, "What don't I know, Daniel?"

Daniel also looked as if he, too, were on the verge of sleep. Like Jenna, he was moving in a gentle rhythm that matched the pattern of Olmigira's rocking.

"I... you see, Jenna, I was, I am worried about you and your... about your restless sleep." He blinked rapidly, as if to clear his vision, and leaned closer. "You looked so ill when I came to see you."

His voice gained strength. "You didn't seem the same—the girl who chased the wind and talked to the trees. Lady Genevieve of the Trees." He said the last in a rush.

Nausea stirred in Jenna's stomach. "You promised Daniel, you promised you wouldn't tell."

Conflicting emotions played across Daniel's face. "I didn't, I mean I was trying to make it into a story, so I could get an idea from Annie. She knows a lot, you see, about healing and spirits and such."

Jenna sat bolt upright, wakened from grogginess by his words. "I never said spirits, Daniel. And you promised. You promised! How could you break your word?"

As bitter tears blurred her vision, she began to quiver with anger at his betrayal.

"Fetch the quilt, boy," Olmigira commanded as she took the tea from Jenna's trembling hands. Daniel placed the quilt around Jenna's shoulders, looking down at her with a stricken face.

Jenna stared at the floor, awash with emotions she didn't know how to handle. After some time, Daniel sat beside her, saying in a shaking voice, "I'm sorry, Jenna, I just wanted to help."

Jenna refused to look at him and nearly missed Olmigira's quiet question.

"What 'tis it that ye need, child?"

"She needs—" Daniel began.

"Hush boy! She must speak her own need."

Jenna's thoughts whirled in confused disorder. How did she answer? She knew what she *wanted*. That was easy enough to say. She wanted to sleep without terror, to roam at will in the meadow, and sit at ease beneath her willow tree, listening to the book bubble beside her, while butterflies gathered on her shoulders.

But her *need?* What did *that* mean?

She looked at the old healer and shook her head slowly. "I don't know." She said it with a heavy sigh. "I don't know what I need."

Olmigira once again started rocking in that steady mesmerizing rhythm, returning to her pipe, the smoke curling about the room in a fragrant dance. Jenna breathed in its pungent odor which made her thoughts heavy and confused. Was that the sea she heard? In a cave? Ah, the slow beat of Olmigira's movement was so like that of the sea. Backward and forward. Backward... and... forward.

"Close your eyes, lass," Olmigira said in more whisper than words.

Jenna's eyelids slowly slid lower, shutting out the light.

"Breathe in the sea," Olmigira whispered. "Go where ye are called."

And she did.

Someone had called her to this now familiar place of darkness. But why was she dressed this way? A long heavy gown of satin, a cape lined with ermine, like costumes from her book of fairy tales. And what was that sound? The distant breaking of waves on a beach?

She became aware that something unwelcome was watching. And waiting.

A cold fear crept around her like a chill fog on a damp autumn night.

Her heart quickened, as though she had been walking at a hurried pace. It was then she saw a shape emerge from the void. A great weight pressed down on Jenna's lungs, making it impossible to breathe, impossible to move.

Her mind screamed, "Run. Hide," yet her heart commanded, "Don't go," for she heard the echo of someone calling her, pleading.

The shape, taking on the form of a shrouded being, moved toward her, its rattling, wheezing breath touching her ears, its voice like a poison. "She thinks you will save her. How sadly mistaken she is. Instead, you will join her, chained, and fettered in a place without hope."

Its white decayed hand reached out toward her arm...

The scream that jerked her awake was not her own.

Jenna's heart pounded in her throat, her breath coming in gasps. Where was Daniel?

Panicked, she looked around, then spotted him, backed against the legs of the worktable, crouched, his eyes full of terror.

That's how I must look when I wake up from my dreams.

She staggered over to him, knelt in front of him, seizing his shoulders. "Daniel, Daniel," she shouted, and shook him.

He didn't seem to see her. Instead, he seemed to be looking inward at a place of darkness.

Horrified, Jenna realized he had somehow followed her into her dream; had seen that appalling being, felt its black wanting, its enveloping malevolence.

"Daniel, it's my dream, my nightmare, you didn't have to look." She trembled with sobs, her eyes stinging.

Has my dream made him blind? Why doesn't he answer?

She held his face in her hands, pleading for him to see her, and was relieved when the terror slowly leeched from his eyes. But when it was replaced by a blank, empty stare, she turned to Olmigira. Waves of rage coursed through Jenna. She stormed across the room, her eyes blazing. Somehow the old woman had conjured up this nightmare.

"Why did you let him enter my dream?"

Olmigira appeared unfazed by Jenna's furious words. "He chose to enter, child. He cares for ye and wants to understand the terror in ye."

"You could have stopped it! Now look at him—he's blind," she screamed with her voice while her mind objected. *Why Jenna, you should be ashamed to be screaming at an old woman.*

Olmigira continued her rocking. "No, child, t'was not my doin'. He chose to look. He will come to hisself in time. He's a brave lad, that one. Fancies himself a knight." Her cackling laugh infuriated Jenna.

"Don't you laugh at him!" The pitch of her voice hurt her head. "Don't you dare laugh at him!" Jenna returned to Daniel's side and, seeing him now drooping in sleep, laid him gently on the floor, covering him with the quilt.

She sat, gently patting his back, whispering, "Daniel, come back please, come back."

Across the room, Olmigira began to sing a soothing lullaby in an unfamiliar language. Like the swirling, hypnotizing clouds from her pipe, the words wrapped themselves around her mind and gradually, imperceptibly lulled her into a place of rest.

It was in the midst of a deep, dreamless sleep that she heard the Night Wind call.

Genevieve, Genevieve Regina, child of the wind, daughter of the woods, come into the velvet blackness of night. She's waiting for you. Come, come.

Blinking, she eased her eyes open to find herself on the bed. The fire had burned to glowing embers, tinting the room the color of late sunset. Daniel still lay in front of the fireplace, only his tousled blond hair visible. From his measured breathing, Jenna knew he was in a deep sleep.

Arising from the bed, she stood in front of Olmigira. In startled surprise Jenna realized that she was dressed in her grandmother's lovely, beaded dress.

"So ye heard it call?" the old healer asked in her scratchy voice.

"Who is waiting for me?"

"It's this way, child. We all o' us are born with a soul full of wondrous beauty. Yet every one of us, as we journey through life, lose a piece o' our soul. Sometimes 'tis stolen, sometimes 'tis just lost for lack of love given or received."

"How would it be stolen?"

"There are those who ha' lost the beauty of their own soul by their greed or hatred or evil deeds and they want after the beauty of other souls. They find ways to deceive and take from them that give into that deceit."

Jenna knelt in front of the rocking chair, listening carefully.

Olmigira's eyes were luminous and wise. "As each grows inta manhood or womanhood, they must find what 'twas lost. If they reach the end o' their livin', and they ha' not found that piece o' soul, then they be condemned ta roam as a spirit, hauntin' the places they had walked in life, still searchin', still seekin'."

"Is there no way for such a spirit to be set free?" Jenna asked, her heart stricken for those condemned to such a fate.

Olmigira nodded gravely. "A personage o' great heart can save a lost soul. One that answers the call of sech a soul can set it free, but great courage be needed. You are sech a one that has been called."

Jenna shivered with a cold that came from deep within her. With trembling words she asked, "What is the courage that is needed to set that soul free?"

Olmigira stopped rocking and looked deep within Jenna's eyes. "Ye must go into that place o' darkness, seek out that evil bein' and look it straight in tha' eyes without blinkin'."

Jenna crumbled into a heap.

Olmigira put her hand under Jenna's chin and lifted her face. "Ye do na have to do it alone."

Relief swelled Jenna's heart. "I can take Daniel?"

"Nay," Olmigira shook her head. "The journey 'tis yourn. He's his own ta make. But the Night Wind has called and will guide ye to that which will help ye."

"It's mid-summer night. It's not safe in the woods," Jenna protested. How could she leave the warmth and safety of Olmigira's cave? "Why am I called to this? Please, don't send me."

"Take out what's in the pocket, girl."

Jenna slowly brought out the iridescent bottle.

"Look child."

The bottle began to glow from within.

"T'will serve as a light to guide yere steps. Go, now, the Night Wind has called."

"But where am I to go?"

"Jus' listen and follow."

"But what of Daniel? How can I leave him behind, lost in some trance?"

"He'll be safely sleepin' here by the fire till ye return. He will awake when ye have completed all ye are called to do."

"He won't awaken if I don't go?" Jenna stared at the old woman, who had painfully eased her arthritic body to a standing position.

"When ye ha' looked the Dark Presence eye-to-eye and ha' na looked away, then Dan'l t'will waken a' your touch upon his shoulder."

Why did you look, Daniel? Her thoughts were angry and bitter. She stood stubbornly unmoving. *She can't force me to go.*

"Nay, I canna force ye to go. 'Tis a task of yere own chosin'."

Jenna hung her head in defeat. What did she care of some lost soul that called her? But if she didn't go, then what of Daniel? It was for Daniel she had to do this impossible thing. And it was Olmigira who had allowed him to fall into this trance.

With hostility in her heart, she walked slowly toward the cave entrance and stood looking out into the woods shrouded in darkness, the wind moaning slightly in the trees. She heard the sound of shuffling feet and then felt the soothing warmth of her cloak around her shoulders.

"Look up, child."

Gazing out above the swaying branches, Jenna saw a night sky alight with thousands of stars. In a sudden flash, she recalled the sultry summer nights of her childhood when her parents took the family to a treeless hill where the heavens with their sparkling lights seemed close enough to touch.

And once again came the Night Wind's call.

Come, it said. *Come.*

The bottle in her hand began to glow.

Behind her, Olmigira said in her crackling voice, "May the wisdom o' the woods go wi' ye child and protect ye in moonlight and starlight, in the dawnin' and the settin' o' the sun."

Jenna felt a gentle squeeze of Olmigira's hands on her shoulders and a gentle nudge. With reluctant steps, Jenna walked out of the cave. As she did, the bottle cast a warm light around her, enabling her to see a short distance ahead.

Refusing to look back at the old woman, Jenna began her unwanted journey, retracing the trail she and Daniel had taken earlier. Soon came the tinkling of tiny bells of the St. Francis shrine. Once there, she saw the shadowed forest track leading back to the mountain.

The way home.

But to her left was the other choice. An unknown way, the way toward that terrifying task Olmigira had set before her. The only way to Daniel's freedom from his dreamless sleep. It was to that way she turned.

She walked slowly, carefully, with the glow of Genevieve's small sea treasure lighting just a few paces in front of her, surrounded by the sounds of the night forest. After a while she no longer gasped when an owl hooted in a distant treetop, nor started, trembling, when a nearby branch creaked in the wind. Frogs croaking by some unseen stream nearby became part of the muted soundscape of the summer woods. And far overhead, the night sky glittered.

She had no measure of passing time as she walked through the darkness but sensed that the spirits of the forest on this mid-summer night meant her no harm.

She became aware that the air was growing colder and settled the cloak more tightly about her, one hand escaping its warmth to hold the light in front of her. After a long while, she noticed the forest becoming less dense, the foliage less thick. She began spotting barren branches, dusted with something reflecting the starlight, the same reflection from the path in front of her.

Puzzled, she knelt to touch the ground, then jumped up, trembling.

It's snow! The height of summer and there's snow. How can this be?

With a few rapid steps, Jenna walked out into an open field under the canopy of the night sky. Beyond the wide field were more woods, but to her right, down a small slope, lay a lake, frozen white and shimmering like diamonds. She noticed a small plank bench next to the iced-over water and in a few moments sat there, tucking her feet under her dress with a grateful sigh. Breathing deeply, she rested with her eyes closed, nearly asleep.

A distant sound startled her.

Caw. Caw.

A raven. High in the trees on the other side of the lake.

As she opened her eyes, Jenna saw something moving in the distance on the ice.

A girl. A girl on skates.

Jenna watched in astonishment as the graceful skater skimmed the ice with ease in slow wide circles and sweeping pirouettes, gradually moved closer and closer.

The skater was dressed all in white—white stockings that clung to the full length of her legs, a sparkling white dress that floated like gentle feathers around her thighs, and a white feather that graced her long, dark curls. She wore a chain of silver, upon which hung a glass key that glistened with the colors of the rainbow whenever the starlight struck it.

She's like a child made of winter.

Drawing to a stop in front of her, the girl held out her hand to Jenna in invitation.

She wants me to skate with her, but I have no skates, and I've never learned how.

As if she heard Jenna's thoughts, the Winter Child, as Jenna named her, gestured to a pair of skates on the other side of the bench.

Is she a fairy? What will happen to me if I go with her?

The Winter Child nodded in encouragement, holding out both her hands.

Caw. Caw.

The unseen raven's voice drifted across the lake, seeming to say *Come. Come.*

Jenna sat up with sudden determination and pulled the skates over her leather slippers, lacing them tightly, then took the girl's extended hands and stood on wobbly legs.

The girl, slightly taller, slid one steadying arm around her waist and guided her forward in small sliding steps. Matching her companion's actions, Jenna soon found her movements grow rhythmic and effortless. At that point, the Winter Child moved her arm from Jenna's waist to provide a sturdy support at her elbow, and eventually just held her hand.

Other than the occasional call of the raven and the swish of their skates, the night was silent. Jenna gave herself up to their effortless, gliding dance across the seamless ice which stirred the deep recesses of her heart, enlivening, awakening, and warming her all at one time.

There was only now. Only this moment. Only this magic night.

Not until the Winter Child slowed their pace, did Jenna realize they were on the other side of the lake, entering the mouth of a stream onto the shimmering, frozen passage that glowed blue-white beneath overhanging branches gleaming with ice.

At last, Jenna felt brave enough to break the silence. "Where are we going?"

The Winter Child's smile was as dazzling as starlight. "A place of great beauty and promise."

"This *is* a place of great beauty," she said firmly in reply.

They skated around a gradual bend to encounter a most stunning obstacle—a glistening wall that stretched to the left, right, and overhead. Within the wall was a door, barely discernible beneath the ice that covered it.

Again, Jenna's companion smiled. "We can see beauty in most every place if we have eyes that know how to look."

As if it had been commanded, the door opened slowly, enabling Jenna and her companion to glide into a small foyer, the walls of which seemed made of frost. Imitating the Winter Child, Jenna sat on a nearby bench of ice and took off her skates.

"One moment, please," the girl said, and disappeared behind a folding screen. After a few moments she emerged, dressed in a full-length white dress with a flowing skirt and sleeves that puffed at the shoulders then narrowed to cover her arms like gloves.

Now she looks like a princess. And not a child.

"Come," the Winter Child said, leading the way through a small door.

Jenna gasped as they entered a brilliantly-lit space. She saw no source of light, yet everything shone. *Our cottage could fit in this one room*, she thought with astonishment.

Benches lined the glistening walls which were covered by huge banners, their brilliant colors muted by a layer of frost. Overhead she saw a high, vaulted ceiling.

This is a castle, Jenna realized with a start. *A castle made of ice.*

Jenna followed the Winter Child to the far end of the room and up three steps to a raised platform. In the center was a circle of pillars, their golden color visible through the layers of frozen water. The pillars surrounded a stone table covered in ice. The only thing on the table was a tiny wooden chest with elaborately embossed leather bindings.

Jenna turned to her companion. "Why have you brought me here?"

The girl in white touched the tiny chest. "Here lies your answer. In here is the weapon you need to conquer the Dark Presence."

When she said the words *Dark Presence*, the Winter Child's voice trembled, as though she could not bear to speak of such a thing. She took the glass key from around her neck and handed it to Jenna, then pointed to the chest.

Jenna stepped up to the mysterious box, her hands shaking. *Olmigira said the Night Wind would guide me to that which will help me. Something in this box will help me face that Dark Presence so I can go back and wake up Daniel.*

Taking a deep breath, she fit the key into the lock and opened the tiny chest.

She stared with stunned surprise at what lay inside. "It's a key," she said, confused, looking at the Winter Child for an answer. "Another key. What sense is that?"

At the other girl's nod, Jenna took out a bronze skeleton key tied on a long red ribbon and held it in her hands, discouragement flooding through her.

"This means there is something else to open, somewhere else to look," she muttered to herself. "Surely there must be something else in here."

She placed the bronze key on the table and examined the little box, looking for a hint, a sign, a note. Something more. But the box held no clues and certainly no answers.

She felt a touch on her arm. The Winter Child looked at her with tenderness.

"Don't lose heart. You have within you the strength for the journey you must take. Think of Daniel, and what he was willing to do for you. You must go on, for your own sake and for the sake of others who await you."

Jenna thought the Winter Child spoke in an odd sing-song rhythm, as though she had memorized a poem to recite at a holiday. "Others? Who, besides Daniel?" Jenna asked in frustration.

The Winter Child smiled sadly. "That I do not know."

"Are you coming with me on my journey?"

A slight shake of the head. "That I cannot do."

"But Olmigira said the Night Wind would lead me to what I needed. Aren't you what I need?"

The girl who seemed made of winter picked up the bronze key and hung it gently around Jenna's neck. "This is what you need. I am but a means to provide it to you."

"Can't you at least tell me your name?"

The girl's eyes glistening with tears. "That I cannot do."

The exhaustion of her night's journey washed over her in a flood, filling Jenna with waves of despair.

After some moments of silence, her companion pointed to Jenna's pocket, then to the doorway through which they had entered. "Go that way. Back out of the castle Take the path to the right; it will lead you into the woods. It is dark, but don't be afraid, you have the light and the key."

"But I don't know what to look for, what to unlock!" Jenna said, dismay filling her voice. How she missed Daniel's cheerful company. "I've just gotten here. Can't I stay?" she pleaded, thinking of the cold night and the dark woods.

The Winter Child touched Jenna's cheek with her hand. "That you cannot do, but don't be disheartened. You've made a good start to your journey. And you will know how to use the key when the time comes."

"I don't have a choice?"

The Winter Child shook her head in a reluctant no.

Jenna wanted to collapse in tears. "I don't want to go."

Jenna didn't want to leave this lovely, sheltered place—enchanted palace or not—nor this girl—be she a fairy or a princess—who felt like a kindred spirit. "Can't I stay just till morning?"

Jenna expected the girl to say, "That you cannot do," but the girl hesitated, clutching her hands.

"I... I... you... don't be disheartened." She repeated the words she had spoken earlier, as if they were a stanza of a poem: "You've made a good start to your journey. And you will know how to use the key when the time comes."

When Jenna didn't move, the Winter Child took her arm tenderly and gently led her down the stairs. The lovely girl was biting her lip as though holding back something she desperately wanted to say. Her face was filled with distress, her eyes sad and longing. In a barely-audible voice she said, "I'm sorry. I'm so sorry."

From somewhere high above in the room came the harsh caw of the raven. Like a warming.

The Winter Child stepped back and took a shaky breath, her eyes wide and startled.

Jenna watched in surprise as the girl all in white scurried back up the steps of the platform, then looked down at Jenna. Standing tall and poised, she pointed regally toward the door. Her stiff demeanor was contradicted by the regret on her face.

Goodbye, she mouthed. *I'll not ever forget you.*

Disconcerted by the Winter Child's actions, Jenna responded with a deep, trembling sigh. "Yes. I shall also remember you, wherever my journey takes me. Goodbye."

Why is everyone always sending me on the way as soon as I arrive?

In minutes, she was outside the Winter Child's ice palace.

It wasn't hard to find the path that turned toward the woods which were eerily silent. No hooting owl. No creaking branches. No croaking frogs. She wished for Daniel's sturdy walking stick to fend off what else she might stumble upon in these woods, for who could say she would encounter someone as welcoming as the Winter Child. Even if she lived in a palace made of ice and gave her a key that unlocked a box holding another key!

It would be so easy to lie down right here and sleep.

She pulled out the iridescent bottle and held it like a torch over her head. It began to glow, and the path became visible for a few feet. Where the light did not reach, the shadows were even darker and more frightening.

She walked and walked and walked until she could walk no more. Bone tired, stumbling from exhaustion, she sat beneath a tree and pulled her cloak close around her.

Above her, the wind, silent for so long, sighed in the trees.

Genevieve.

Jenna sat up taller, looking around. Everywhere was thick, heavy darkness. "Who called?"

Genevieve Regina.

"Is it the Night Wind who calls?"

She stood up and held the sea-green bottle over her head like a beacon in a lighthouse. It shed a circle of luminescence around her, but there was no person, no being in sight. *At least nothing I can see with my eyes.*

The voice had been so clear. Much clearer than in her dreams.

Tucking the bottle in her pocket, she snuggled deeper into her cloak. Remembering Daniel's stories about staying overnight in the woods, she gathered a pile of leaves and pine needles to make a soft bed, then piled more on top of herself as a blanket. She curled into a tight ball, cradling her head on her hands.

Goodnight, Daniel. I hope you are safe in Olmigira's cave.

A distant sound reached her ears. Was that a raven? Too weary to be afraid, she gave herself up to sleep.

6

A CASTLE ON THE HILL

When Jenna awoke, it was morning. Though the forest floor was dim, she could see blue sky through a few openings in the trees. No trace of snow remained on the ground or overhead branches and the temperature was that of early spring.

Have I left the Winter Child's kingdom?

She stood up, brushing off her blanket of leaves, then fingered the key around her neck to be sure her encounter with the Winter Child hadn't been a dream. Her stomach protested with a hungry gurgle.

But Olmigira gave me no food for the journey.

A more brightly lit area in the far distance to her right caught her attention. A clearing in the woods? A homestead? Walking off the path might not be a wise thing, but her hunger was too great to ignore, so she plunged into the undergrowth.

Struggling through the shrubs, intertwined saplings, and vine-covered fallen trees made for slow progress. But before long she saw a break in the trees and the forest floor began to open up.

Walking became less cumbersome and soon she was practically running toward the clearing ahead.

The woods ended abruptly, and Jenna found herself in a field of shimmering wheat under a bright azure sky. The golden field danced as though it were playing with the wind. The scent of spring, the chirp of crickets, and call of the sparrow filled the air. Breathing in the air and light, Jenna spun around in circles, laughing softly. *Daniel would call me Genevieve of the Breeze.*

A half-mile or so distant, she spotted movement in a grove of trees.

People? Maybe they'll have something to eat.

She began to race across the field until an unnerving thought stopped her.

Not everyone I meet on this journey is going to be as welcoming at the Winter Child. After all, this was a journey to find The Dark Presence. As if in contradiction to that terrifying thought, the wind delivered a lilting melody of young girls singing and the unexpected scent of ripe, luscious fruit.

With a sudden burst of excitement, she doubled her pace across the expanse of yellow toward the small stand of flowering trees. Drawing near, she saw three girls in a patch of wildflowers dancing in a circle. Their words were beautifully sung, but in a language Jenna did not recognize. When she halted at edge of the fruit-laden trees, the barefoot girls paused to look at her, hands still linked.

They wore identical dresses, but in different colors: white, yellow, and peach. A wreath of flowers perched on their yellow-white hair and a belt of vines twined about their waists. From their varying heights, Jenna guessed they were about ten, eleven, and twelve years of age.

And so beautiful.

Jenna, suddenly weak from hunger and exertion, collapsed in the flowers, her head spinning.

The girls called in alarm to each other in the language she did not understand. One picked up a tankard and ran for water at the nearby spring. Another pulled out bread and cheese from a tightly-woven basket. The third plucked several pieces of round orange fruit from an overhanging branch.

Converging on her at once, chattering in concerned tones, they offered their gifts urgently. Jenna smiled in woozy appreciation. She drank the bone-chilling water eagerly and made quick work of the crusty bread and mellow cheese. The fruit was unlike anything she had ever eaten—sweet, dripping of juice, with neither pits nor seeds.

As she ate, the girls carried on an animated conversation. Though she didn't know what they were saying, it was clear they were talking about her. Finally refreshed, Jenna looked at them, hoping she could make herself understood.

"My name is Jenna."

They stopped at once, looking at her intensely.

"Jenna, what a beautiful name," the oldest, dressed in peach, said with a smile.

Jenna blinked. Although the girl continued speaking the language Jenna did not know, she understood the words.

The yellow-gowned girl giggled. "No one is ever the same after they eat from our fruit tree. And you have the gift of understanding." She pointed to the key which hung about Jenna's neck.

The youngest, in white, nodded. "Anyone who wears a key holds great power." Then she curtsied. "My name is Innocence. This is my sister, Wonder, and that is my sister, Delight."

Wonder, in peach, twirled. Delight, in yellow, smiled radiantly.

Jenna thought the names suited each of them perfectly "Where do you live?"

Wonder pointed to a hill in the distance. To Jenna's astonishment, it was topped by a castle that looked like a picture in a storybook. Had it been there before?

"We live there," Wonder explained, "and every morning we come here to spend the day."

"And every night," Delight said, "we go back to the castle."

Jenna sensed some underlying sadness in Delight's statement, but how could anyone who lived in a castle at the edge of such a beautiful field be unhappy.

"Jenna, do you want to dance with us?" Innocence asked, jumping up. "We can teach you our songs, and you can teach us yours."

In the cool shade of the grove, Jenna danced and sang the day away with her new friends. When they grew tired, they picked the strange but delightful orange-hued fruit or walked barefoot through the icy-cold stream.

Jenna sang words to songs she had never heard, did not understand, but somehow knew.

"*E wac hauoi noch, les te noiah boch. Aie alouie yoch, oiah, oiah loch.*"

As the day waned, they sat in a circle, and the three girls began to hum a soothing melody, soon adding words. Jenna closed her eyes, pulled into a state of mellow contentment by their voices.

> *A thousand stars light up the night*
> *and paint the heart with wonder.*
> *She stands in awe before the sight;*
> *her mind has much to ponder.*
>
> *She walks among the golden wheat,*
> *plucks shafts for wreaths entwining,*
> *Picks kernels ripened in the heat,*
> *for on the millstone grinding.*
>
> *She never stops or halts her gaze*
> *at all the beauty 'round her*
> *for nature's wondrous, bounteous ways*
> *enrich her days with wonder.*

The music faded as she opened her eyes. Wonder knelt before her, holding a bouquet of wheat in her hand. Jenna took the golden offering, laid it on her lap, sitting as the others, silent and at ease.

But when the wind began to rustle the leaves, Wonder suddenly leapt up. "We've lingered too long in our orange grove. Hurry!"

Alarmed at the edge of panic in Wonder's voice, Jenna realized she hadn't told them about her search nor asked if her key fit any lock they knew of. In a matter of minutes, the three girls had slipped on their shoes, gathered their things, and started toward the castle, which now loomed dark and foreboding in the red glow of the sinking sun.

"Wait," Jenna called after them, frantically looking for her cloak.

"The sun is setting," Delight yelled back over her shoulder. "Innocence, Wonder, you must go faster."

Even from a distance, Jenna heard an edge of fear in Delight's voice.

The other sisters quickened their pace.

Jenna spotted her cloak behind a tree, grabbed it, and raced after them. "Stop!" she shouted. "Wait. Please, wait for me."

Did they expect me to stay out here in the dark? Why does everyone I meet send me on my way just as I get to know them?

Innocence, trailing the others, turned to look at Jenna.

"Can't you wait?" Jenna called to her.

"No," the littlest sister yelled back. "He will come for us if we've not returned by sunset."

"He?" They mentioned no "he" during their delightful day together. Tossing the bouquet of wheat to the ground, she gathered up her skirt and put on a burst of speed. "Stop, please stop. Let me stay the night. I don't want to be out here by myself."

The three girls halted abruptly, and Jenna, breathless, caught up to them a moment later.

Wonder stared at her with wide eyes and raised eyebrows. "You want to come into the castle? But you don't have to. You can stay out here in the field and the grove."

Jenna shook her head, trying to explain between breaths. "No... it's lonely out... here."

"If you came in with us, where would you sleep?" Innocence questioned. She too seemed puzzled at Jenna's desire to come with them.

They have a huge castle, and they have no room for a guest?

"She could come into our chamber," Wonder said tentatively.

"I won't be any trouble, I promise," Jenna pleaded. The thought of another night alone, be it in the woods or an open field, filled her with dread. "I'd be glad to clean or cook or anything. Just, please, don't leave me out here alone."

Innocence put her hand on Jenna's arm and said to the others, "I don't know why she would rather come into the castle, but we cannot leave her here alone if she does not want to be."

Jenna was surprised to see tears on the young girl's face.

"Yes!" Delight stamped her foot, making her yellow dress bounce. "Yes!"

Wonder nodded. "Yes. We can do this. Two of us can distract the guards and the other sneak her down into our chamber.

Once she's there, we will all be safe. She can share tea, and in the morning, she can go on her way."

The suggestion to "distract the guards" and "sneak her into the chamber" alarmed Jenna.

"Don't people come to visit you?" she asked. Their lack of hospitality seemed so out of character. *Perhaps there is a good reason I should not go with them into the castle.*

"Yes," Innocence said, her voice barely a whisper, "once, a very, very long time ago, a young woman"—she paused to peer at Jenna intensely—"a stranger..."

"Stop!" Wonder shouted. "You mustn't..."

Delight covered her ears, as though afraid of what would come next.

Innocence's eyes glittered with unshed tears. "She came into the castle, and she's never left."

Delight was wringing her hands, moaning. "Don't, don't, you mustn't tell her. Innocence, come, you must come now. We're going to go find a way to distract the guards."

She and Wonder started running ahead. But Innocence, seemingly oblivious to the others' dismay, stood looking at Jenna, adding in a puzzled voice, "There is a thing that is so odd, so strange indeed."

A fiery anxiety creep into Jenna's veins. *I should probably leave. Go back to the woods, find the path again.*

"Yes," Innocence continued. "Yes. It's odd, you see, for you have the look of her."

Jenna wanted to cover her ears with her hands like Delight had done.

"And her name reminds me of yours, you see," Innocence said in a contemplative tone, then abruptly spurted after her sisters.

Jenna's mind spun like a top on a table. *Why does everyone speak in riddles or leave half-said clues? Why can't anyone make sense?*

Innocence's voice drifted on the wind to Jenna. "Jenna. Isn't that short for Genevieve?"

Jenna stood stunned, staring at the fleeing girls whose frantic actions were in stark contrast to their afternoon of leisure. Then, in a burst of determination, she raced after them toward the castle, which grew bleaker as it loomed closer. Sinister turrets reached high above the castle walls at each corner. No welcoming light beckoned; no encouraging host awaited.

The sun had sunk behind the horizon and daylight was quickly fading from the sky when Jenna caught up with the girls at the drawbridge. They were gathered in a circle, whispering fiercely in agitated tones.

"I won't be a burden," Jenna said in an apologetic tone, trying not to show the growing anxiety their hesitancy had unleashed in her. They were clearly taking a risk by bringing her into the castle for the night. What were they afraid of?

"We are decided?" Delight asked.

The other two nodded.

"We must hurry for the drawbridge will be pulled up any minute," Delight urged, then said to Jenna, "You must hide here for a bit. We will go in and distract the guards, and then I will come get you. But you must not be seen. It would be a bad thing to be caught."

I wonder if this Genevieve had been "caught."

Jenna crouched among the bushes at the edge of the drawbridge, wrapping her cloak around her against the sudden plunge in temperature. The wait seemed interminable. To distract herself, she pictured Daniel sitting at her family's table regaling them with his entertaining stories. She did not want to remember the look of terror on his face when she had awoken from her dream in Olmigira's cave.

"Daniel," she whispered, "why do I have to do this alone?"

From across a distance too far to be measured in miles, she heard a faint whisper. Maybe it was no more than the wind rattling the bush or the swish of a nearby bird taking flight, but it felt like an answer, as if he thought of her in his dreamless state.

The sudden tap of footsteps crossing the drawbridge jerked Jenna's mind back to her precarious position. Mindful of guards, she stooped lower.

"Jenna!"

She looked up to see Delight. "We must hurry."

Delight caught her hand and led her rapidly across the drawbridge, past the open iron-clad wooden doors, and into the passageway between the doors and the inner wall. She pressed Jenna against the cold stone surface. Jenna looked up to see a thick iron gate raised overhead. The portcullis. She remembered Daniel explaining it could be lowered to prevent intruders from entering the castle if they made it through the outer doors.

"The guards would shoot arrows down on them or pour boiling oil on them through the openings in the ceiling above."

Jenna had shuddered at Daniel's vivid descriptions of castle warfare. During their stay with Annie, he talked endlessly about the time of knights and ladies.

"But Daniel," she had said, "nobody lives in castles anymore. I've only ever seen the ruins by the river where my willow tree is."

"The King lives in a castle in faraway London," he replied.

"But there aren't knights in armor anymore, are there? The soldiers have muskets and gunpowder, and their leaders ride horses in fancy red uniforms."

"There will be knights and ladies in the books I write," Daniel insisted.

"Look, isn't it delightful!" Delight's giggle drew Jenna's attention to the middle of the large dirt courtyard where Innocence and Wonder were singing and dancing in front of a seated man dressed in a faded blue tunic and tight-fitting leggings. A long, treacherous-looking sword lay on the ground beside him. Their song was eerie and entrancing. He stared at the dancers, transfixed.

"Come, quickly," Delight whispered again. She pulled Jenna around the corner to the right and some distance along the wall.

As they moved, Jenna's eyes were drawn to the towers across the courtyard. The turret on the left was dark, its windows no more than slits in the stones. But in the tower to the right, light was seeping out of the narrow openings near the pointed, conical roof. She spotted a man walking along the parapet atop the castle wall just below the tower. He didn't seem to notice the girls dancing in the courtyard or the seated guard.

If these are the guards, they're not doing a very good job. She wasn't sure the thought was comforting or disconcerting.

"Here. In here." Delight urged her into an open doorway and across a small landing. "Follow me!" she whispered, then dashed down a flight of winding stairs inside the circular tower.

Jenna followed at a slower pace. It was so dim she had to feel her way along the cold, damp stone wall, straining to see the next narrow triangular step. Round and round she went, the air increasingly damp.

Finally, a flickering light appeared as the stairs emptied onto the intersection of two corridors dimly lit by candlesticks burning in wall sconces. A few feet down the passageway to the left Jenna saw a large wooden door. A set of large skeleton keys hung nearby on the wall.

"Here, hide here," Delight urged, indicating a recessed niche beneath the last turn of the stairs. "Don't move. Don't make a sound."

Her heart pounding at Delight's insistent tone, Jenna pressed herself into the cramped space. From her vantage point, she could see neither the bottom of the stairs nor the other passageway.

Where did Delight go?

Her doubts about the wisdom of entering the castle grew rapidly. What of this "he" who would "come get them" if they did not return to the castle by sunset? It felt like a long time until she heard footsteps clambering down the stone stairs and recognized the voices of Innocence, Wonder, and Delight. But instead of stopping to get her, they hurried past her hiding space. In a moment, the creak of hinges and the slam of a door echoed down the hallway.

Jenna's heart pounded against her chest. *Did they forget me?*

The sound of marching feet to her right sent a breath-stealing chill up her spine, and she pressed herself as deep as she could into the small crevice. She guessed there were two or three guards whose footsteps paused a short distance down the passageway. A door groaned open, and a man announced in a gruff voice, "Here are your fixings for tea, young ladies."

He sounds kind. Not at all like a fierce or fearsome guard.

After a few minutes, the men left the chamber, came past her hiding space, and went down the other passageway, their treading feet fading in the distance.

In another minute, Jenna heard Delight's frantic voice. "Jenna, come."

Jenna followed Delight down the hall, through the open door, and into a chamber. Delight pulled the door closed behind them with a soft thump.

She had expected a dungeon, but instead she was in a cozy, comfortable room. A roaring fire in a huge walk-in fireplace lit the chamber with light and warmth. The contents of a black kettle bubbled over the fire, filling the air with a savory and rich scent. A large, braided rug in shades of blue lay on the floor in front of the fireplace.

On the mantle, a purple vase filled with pink, yellow, and white wildflowers added a homey touch. A beautiful tapestry depicting a blooming garden walkway with a bench and overhanging trees covered the wall above the mantle.

On one side of the fireplace, a small bookshelf displayed several leather-bound books, toys, and writing implements. On the other side, four wooden chairs surrounded a small table covered with a lace runner. The table was set with a china teapot and dainty cups painted with violets, plus crockery plates and cutlery. In the middle, a tray of inviting baked treats rested next to a jar of fruit preserves. A long bench strewn with small, embroidered pillows stood against the wall behind the table.

Jenna turned around to take in the rest of the chamber. A large chifforobe—a wooden clothes closet—flanked by two additional chairs took up most of the wall to the left of the door. At the other end of the room, the beds were made up with brightly flowered coverlets and huge fluffy pillows. Daintily dressed cloth dolls perched on the beds identifying their owners by the colors of their outfits—peach, yellow, and white.

"Why is there a fourth bed and a doll in green?" Jenna asked as she turned to the girls who were watching her with welcoming smiles. "Yes," Innocence said. "There are four sisters."

"But who is the fourth sister?"

"That is Joy. She was summoned to the tower this morning, just as we were on our way to the meadow," Delight explained.

"Summoned?" Jenna thought the word ominous. "By who?"

"The boy."

Wonder's terse reply was not very helpful. "What boy?" Jenna persisted.

"He doesn't have a name. We call him the Boy in the Tower," Innocence replied, shedding no light on his identity. At Jenna's perplexed look, Innocence continued. "We have only seen him at a distance. He sometimes stands on the balcony outside his tower, watching us come and go from the grove. He's older, I think, maybe older than Joy. Even from a distance you can tell he's a very sour boy."

"Sour boy?" Jenna chuckled.

"Oh yes," Delight said solemnly. "He never smiles. Takes delight in nothing."

"Why was Joy summoned to the tower?" Jenna asked. It was so confusing—a fortress with boy they'd never met who lived in an area they had never seen. Were they prisoners? There were guards, after all. Yet they didn't live in a dungeon. And where were their parents?

"We don't know why she was sent for," Wonder said with a heavy sigh. "None of us have ever gone to the tower before."

"Are you worried about him? The boy?" Jenna probed. "Is he the one who will come get you if you don't come in?"

Innocence tittered. "The Boy in the Tower? Oh, no, we're not afraid of *him*." Then her face saddened. "We're just afraid Joy might not return for a long time, like before." The last words were said so softly, Jenna could barely hear them.

Jenna tried to sort it out. "You're not afraid of the Boy in the Tower, but you're afraid Joy might not return, like before? But she's never been to the tower?"

"No, like before when we went to see the Woman Who Wails in the Night."

"The who!?"

"Innocence, you musn't talk of her," Delight said in an urgent voice.

Innocence ignored her sister. "Genevieve," the youngest sister said. "She said her name is Genevieve Regina."

Jenna felt a wave of dizziness wash over her, and she sat suddenly on one of the chairs.

"See, you've frightened her," Wonder scolded her sister.

Jenna looked at each of the three sisters in turn. "Tell me about her," she demanded.

The others looked shocked at the sudden change in Jenna's demeanor.

"I must know!" She softened her voice. "It's very important."

"Well, yes," Wonder replied hesitantly. "Let's have tea, and we'll tell you about her. Though Joy will be most put out by us. But first take off your cloak and hang it in the wardrobe."

The tea was hot, sweet, and soothing. The four of them quietly ate their afternoon treat until Delight said, "Here is what we know."

Jenna eyed her across the table and waited.

"It was a very long time ago... I think," Delight looked at Innocence and Wonder, who nodded in agreement.

"But," Jenna interrupted, "if it was a very long time ago, how can you remember? You're all younger than me. You must have been very little if it was a *very* long time ago."

Innocence shook her head. "No," she replied. "I think I was this age."

"How could you be this age, if it was a very long time ago?" Jenna asked, baffled.

Innocence shrugged. "I don't know. It's not important."

I think it's rather important, Jenna thought. *But no one seems to be willing or able to explain these important things to me.*

"I'm sorry, go on," Jenna urged Delight, who had been interrupted by this conversation about what "a very long time ago" meant.

"Yes, well..." Delight paused to gather her thoughts. "It was a strange day. Storm clouds had gathered in the west and blew in from the sea."

"The sea?" Jenna almost shouted. "There's a sea nearby?"

"It's been a long time since we've seen the sea. It's west of the castle," Innocence replied.

"Yes," Wonder said, her eyes closed, her voice filled with awe. "The waves crash on the beach, the air blows all the time, and marvelous treasures to find…"

"May I continue with my story?" Delight frowned, clearly not delighted at being interrupted constantly. "I can't tell a story if it isn't listened to."

Jenna wondered how far she could have come from Olmigira's cave in one night's walk through the woods. *This could be a world from Daniel's imaginings.*

"Ah-hem." Delight sat with her arms crossed over her yellow dress, her foot tapping the floor, staring at her.

Jenna settled back in her chair. "Oh, yes, I'm ready to listen."

"As I said, it was a strange day. Storm clouds had gathered in the west, but they were a sick greenish yellow hue, not a lovely cloud color."

"Like peach," Wonder interjected pertly. "Peach is a lovely cloud color."

"Yes, Wonder," Delight sighed. "That is a lovely cloud color. However, these clouds were not peach."

"I don't know if you should call the clouds sick," Innocence said, frowning. "They had green and yellow in them; those are nice colors."

Delight sighed again. "I said they were sick looking, a greenish yellow. Not that green or yellow are not nice colors, but there's a certain way they mix together." She stopped and looked pointedly at everyone.

Innocence smiled brightly and Wonder nodded.

Delight addressed Jenna, looking at her alone. "As I was saying, we were going to come in early from the meadow because the day was so odd looking. Mind you, we hate coming back before nightfall, but sometimes we will if it's one of those..." She paused.

"What?" Jenna urged, leaning in. "One of those what?"

Delight said quietly in Jenna's ear, "Evil days."

Jenna sat back suddenly, nearly knocking herself over.

"Oh, Jenna, be careful." Innocence exclaimed, clutching at Jenna.

"Has Delight's story upset you, Jenna? Here, have another cup of tea." Wonder poured more of the strong, sweet brew.

"I'm only telling the story," Delight said, not at all apologetic. "It's how the story goes, and I have to tell it all."

"No, it's all right," Jenna insisted, clutching the cup of tea. "Please, I'll be fine. I want to hear the story. I won't interrupt again."

Delight glared at Innocence and Wonder.

"Neither will we," they chimed together.

"Let's see. Oh, yes," Delight began, apparently loving to tell a tale. "It was an..." she paused for dramatic effect "...evil day."

When no one interrupted, she continued. "The sky was full of strange colors, and the clouds looked frightened. The birds chirped an odd song. Nothing was right. Even the air had a smell of foreboding." Delight smiled, appearing pleased with her vivid descriptions.

"By sunset, the sky everywhere was full of thick, greenish black clouds, piled high up on top of each other, like clouds do before a thunderstorm. But these clouds were not the wondrous, puffy white clouds that turn into a gray warning."

"Ah, the clouds before a thunderstorm are—" Wonder began but was silenced by a glare from Delight.

"By the time we got to the castle it had started to storm. Terrible thunder and lightning. Sharp, horrid cracks and frightful jags of lightning everywhere. One hit the tree in the courtyard just as we came through the castle doors. It was terrifying."

Jenna remembered the withered tree in the middle of the courtyard where Innocence and Wonder had distracted the guard.

"We were shaking from fear, well, except Wonder. She just kept oohing and ahhing at everything. We had to drag her away from the sight of the wild clouds and the burning tree and hurry down to our room. Even in our beds with the covers over our heads, we could still hear the wind howling like a lost child, and thunder rattling our china. We thought it would never end."

Wonder and Innocence appeared enthralled by the story, as though it were the first time they had ever heard it.

"Finally, after a long, long, long time"—Delight stopped, looking at each of them.

Jenna tried not to smile at Delight's fanciful storytelling.

—"the storm began to die down. The wind quieted a bit, and the thunder rumbled just in the distance. That's when we heard it."

Jenna waited, impatiently, sipping her tea, but it was clear that Delight wouldn't be hurried.

"The weeping," Wonder spoke up softly, looking as if she just now remembered it. "We heard the weeping."

"Yes," Innocence agreed. "We didn't know what to do. Someone was crying so sadly, with a broken heart." Big tears fell one by one down Innocence's cheeks.

Wonder patted Innocence's hand sympathetically and murmured a gentle word, saying as she did, "Even Joy was upset, and there's not much that upsets her."

Delight went on with her tale. "We didn't think there was much we could do, because the guards always lock our door after they take away our supper. But that night the door wasn't locked." Delight shook her head, as if still surprised.

"Yes," Innocence agreed. "It was open, and Joy said we should go find the Woman Who Wails in the Night."

"How did you know it was a woman?" Jenna asked.

"You could tell," Wonder replied, sighing. "It was a girl's weeping. After all, we're girls, and we know the sound of a girl crying."

Delight continued. "We crept out into the passageway and from there could tell which way the sobbing came from. It was in a direction we had never been before."

"You see," Innocence interjected, "we aren't allowed to go anywhere without the guards, except out to the grove and the wheat field."

They truly must be prisoners or captives of some sort.

"Joy led the way," Delight was saying. "We crept after her in our nightgowns and bare feet. The floor was like ice." She paused to pour everyone a fresh cup of tea.

Wonder picked up the story. "We walked until the passageway ran into another one with a stairway like the one near our chamber. We turned down that passageway, following the sound of her crying, which grew louder and louder. Somewhere along the hall we came upon a stairway leading further down."

Jenna saw the fear on Wonder's face and heard it in her voice.

"We didn't want to go," the girl said, "because there was no light down there, and even with our candles..." She paused and dropped her eyes, her fists clenched.

"There is..." Delight spoke in a solemn voice. "The... Keeper... you see."

"We know he dwells somewhere in the castle, but we never see him," Innocence explained in a loud whisper.

Wonder added softly, leaning toward Jenna, "Except for—"

"Things are nice here," Delight said in a rush. "We have lovely things to eat and lovely days in the meadow."

"And our chamber is cozy, and the beds are warm," Wonder proclaimed.

"But..." Jenna prompted.

"But," Delight picked up, "we must always be in our chamber by nightfall. We must never wander around on our own. We must never go to the tower. And we must never, never, never…"

"Go into the dungeon." Innocence finished so quietly Jenna had to strain to hear.

The room seemed to hold its breath until Jenna asked, "Is that where Genevieve was?"

Delight looked over her shoulder, then said in a conspiratorial tone, "There was a time, a long time ago when… The Keeper… when he came and told us the rules."

Jenna felt a nauseous twist in her stomach. "So, you were here before The Keeper came?"

Delight's face was a study in concentration. "I think. Well, I don't know. Some things we can remember, like this story, but others are all so hazy, cloudy, full of fog. It hurts to remember."

"What does…" Jenna hesitated to say the name, "…The Keeper look like?" It was a question she didn't want to ask, but knew she had to.

The three sisters looked at one another warily.

"We don't ever like to think about… that being," Innocence explained, her voice quavering, her face paler than her white dress.

Delight put a comforting hand on her youngest sister's arm and said to Jenna, "The Keeper is a spirit that wears a black cloak to give it form, but it has no form, no substance." Her voice began to quaver. "And its breath is—"

"—like a hollow rattling in your ear." Jenna finished in a rush as she leapt to her feet, sending her chair crashing backwards to the floor.

The sisters sprung to Jenna's side.

"You've seen The Keeper and you've never been here before!" Delight's voice was full of astonishment.

"She has a key," Wonder reminded the others.

Delight put her arm around Jenna's trembling shoulders, leading her across the room and seating her on one of the beds. "Come, lie down on my bed."

Innocence took off Jenna's shoes. They settled Jenna against the pillows and tucked her under the coverlet, then sat near her, surrounding her with their comforting presence. Wonder brought her another cup of tea, and they waited while Jenna slowly drank the soothing beverage.

Then Wonder asked, "Shall I continue the story?"

Jenna gave a slow nod.

"We knew that going to the dungeon was forbidden," Wonder said. "But Joy said we could not leave so needy a soul alone without comfort. I couldn't think of anything at all delightful down there in the darkness, and I didn't want to go, but Joy insisted. She held the candle above her head, and we crept down the stairs, one by one." There was awe in her voice at this terrible, wonderful thing they did.

"The smell was of dead things and putrid water," Innocence added, shuttering. "There was no air. You could hardly breathe."

If only I had their courage, Jenna thought, looking at them with new eyes.

"At last, we reached the bottom stair," Delight said, "and—"

Bam!

The slam of the chamber door against the outside wall sent them all into a screaming panic. Innocence flung herself under one of the beds. Wonder crouched behind another. Delight stood as one turned to stone, shielding Jenna from view.

Jenna slunk beneath the covers, trembling.

She'd been discovered.

7

THE VOICE IN THE NIGHT

From beneath the covers, Jenna heard the unexpected sound of girlish giggles and squeals of excitement. Disconcerted, she peaked her head out to see Delight run across the room and fling herself on someone standing just inside the door. Delight was quickly joined by Wonder and Innocence.

The three girls danced around the newcomer with glee, obscuring Jenna's view.

"The door!" Delight shouted in sudden alarm. She moved the others out of the way and closed out the darkness of the corridor, restoring the seclusion of their chamber and giving Jenna a first glimpse of the unexpected visitor.

She wore the same dress as the others, but in the pale green of a newly bloomed meadow on a soft spring day. Her face was lit up with a wide smile and her eyes sparkled with merriment.

This was obviously Joy, the fourth sister. The oldest.

"Who is that!" Joy's demeanor turned to alarm as she spotted Jenna.

Delight pulled her oldest sister across the room. "It's Jenna. Isn't she lovely? We found her outside. Or rather she found us in the grove. She was faint with hunger, so we gave her some bread and fruit and sang and danced all afternoon. It was delightful! She didn't want to stay outside in the dark at sunset, so we brought her inside."

As Delight stopped to catch her breath, Wonder took up the story with just as much excitement. "Delight snuck her inside while Innocence and I entranced the guard with our song. It was ever so much fun, like it used to be."

"Yes," Innocence agreed. "It was ever so much fun," she said, giving Joy a guileless look.

Jenna began to wonder if Innocence weren't a bit cunning beneath her naive air.

"And we were telling her about the Woman Who Wails in the Night—"

"What!?" Joy's thunderous response belied her name. "You were what?!" She glared at Jenna with outrage. "I demand you tell me right now who you are and how you tricked them into bringing you in the castle when they know it is forbidden."

The three girls looked at Jenna sheepishly.

Jenna thought if Joy had been with her sisters earlier, Jenna would still be outside in the dark, alone.

"You needn't yell." Jenna sat up and stared back at Joy. "My name is Jenna and your sisters... well, I did ask them to bring me inside." Jenna tried not to sound as if she was confessing something shameful. "If I've done anything wrong, I'm sorry. But I was afraid."

Joy looked as though nothing could frighten her.

"There was another reason I wanted to enter the castle," Jenna went on. "I heard about Genevieve. It doesn't make any sense, but I think this is impossible, but... she may be my grandmother."

The girls gaped at Jenna, speechless. Even Joy looked taken aback.

Jenna smiled inwardly at having gained the upper hand over the older sister, who Jenna guessed was about her own age.

With an indrawn breath, Wonder shouted, "Tell us!"

"Yes, tell us," Innocence begged. "Let us all sit here by Jenna and hear her story."

The three younger girls gathered on Jenna's bed and the one nearby.

Jenna replied, "Before I tell my story, you must finish your story about the night you went to see the Woman Who Wails in the Night."

"What about my story of visiting the Boy in the Tower?" Joy demanded, clearly annoyed at no longer being the center of attention. "I have a great deal to tell." She glowered at Jenna as she plunked down on the bed across from Jenna.

"She's right, Joy." Delight contradicted her older sister. "Let me finish the story *I* was telling, and then Jenna can tell *hers*. And then you must tell *yours*, because no one will want to interrupt *your* story. It will be the *most* interesting."

"It's very foolish to speak of the Woman Who Wails in the Night," Joy muttered, but didn't interrupt again as Delight continued her story.

"We just got to the part where we reached the bottom of the stairway," Delight explained to Joy and then looked back at Jenna. "As I was saying, at the bottom of the stairway there was a hallway with several doors, each of which had an opening filled with iron bars. All the cells were dark, but the weeping led us to her chamber."

Jenna sat attentively, watching Delight.

"A set of keys hung by the doorpost, which Joy used to open the lock."

Jenna could picture the four of them, pulling the heavy wooden door open.

"Joy held up her candle so we could see the steps down to the cell floor," Delight explained. "It was damp and cold and smelled horrid. In the center of the cell was a pile of straw and a pillar, and there was the weeping woman chained to the pillar by leg irons."

"Oh, Jenna," Innocence said mournfully. "She was on her knees, bent over, weeping and weeping. Never in all my life have I heard such crying. As if every joy had been taken from her."

"We crept down the stairs and across the cell," Delight went on. "I didn't want to think about what we were stepping on." She shuddered at the memory. "The woman was so caught up in her wailing that she didn't look up until Innocence touched her shoulder."

"She was a young woman," Innocence added.

"And she had long, beautiful hair, like yours," Delight continued. "Delightfully curly, but it was full of straw and, strangely enough, sand."

Jenna felt a tightness growing in her chest.

"She did not seem surprised to see us but continued to sob. I asked her who she was, and she said her name was Genevieve. I asked her why she was in the dungeon." Delight stopped, looking cautiously at Jenna.

"Let me tell," Wonder said.

"Yes, go ahead," Delight assented, relief on her face.

Wonder said, "She suddenly stopped weeping and stared at us, one by one, and then in the saddest voice I've ever heard, she told this story."

My Jacob's a captain, you see. So handsome. But always at sea. I was a married woman with no husband to take me to the gatherings, festivities, and seaside picnics I had so delighted in as a girl. So, one day, when I was invited to a party, I went, much against my older sister's wishes.

I didn't care if she thought I was being scandalous, going without an escort, as my brothers were away. Nor did I listen when Myra said baby Joanna was unusually fussy, and I ignored little Jacob who begged me to read him a bedtime story.

At the party, I encountered an old beau. He was a handsome soldier in a dashing black cape. He asked me if I wanted to walk on the beach.

Wonder took Jenna's hand in hers. "The woman had a terrible haunted look to her, and she began to weep again, great sobbing, wailing cries. I could barely keep from weeping with her."

Delight took Jenna's other hand, her eyes full of sadness. "Oh, Jenna, it's so sad, you see for when she got home, she found that the baby had died."

"But there's more, Jenna," Wonder said in hesitant tone, and continued Genevieve's story.

I woke from some kind of hazed sleep and found myself walking on the beach. My head ached, and my throat burned, and I trembled with exhaustion. Something was wrong. Terribly wrong and then, then I remembered. The baby. My wee little girl.

I was suddenly filled with a rage so overpowering that I wanted to tear my hair out. But then, I thought, no, it's not me. It's not my fault. It's Jacob. Yes, his fault. He's the one... if he hadn't always been at sea, if he had been there, little Joanna...

And then overcome by a thirst to punish him, I knelt down in front of the sea and screamed out across the waves, "You love the sea more than you have ever loved me. Or your children. So let your true mistress embrace you. Let her pull you down into her depths where you will never be parted from the one you love most."

Delight took up the story in a trembling voice. "She said she woke up here, in the dungeon. And there was a presence, a being, covered in a black cloak, its face hidden, its voice terrifying. It told her he had granted her wish. That the sea had claimed Jacob and all of his crew, but she would have to pay the price of her own soul in exchange for that of the men who had perished."

Silence suddenly descended on the room as if those sitting there hoped that the walls could absorb the sorrow of such a saga and keep the hearts of those listening from being torn asunder.

In that space of quiet, Jenna tried to take in the incomprehensible story, similar to the one Aunt Myra had told. How could it be that Genevieve was in this castle? In a dungeon? Was she alive? What was this place Jenna had wandered into?

Jenna felt suddenly overwhelmed and sank back onto the bed, her eyes closed.

She heard the sisters whisper intensely.

"Poor Jenna, she's quite overcome." There were tears in Innocence's voice.

"But the guards will be here soon with supper." Joy was commanding.

Delight piped up. "I'll hide under the bed, and we can pretend I'm sick with the ague. They'll never guess!"

Wonder chimed in. "Yes, that's a marvelous idea, Delight. Go quickly, I hear the guards coming."

Jenna heard shuffling feet. Her heart beat with alarm.

"Wonder, make sure her hair is covered with the blanket, or they'll see she has ebony locks, not flaxen ones," Joy ordered.

Jenna felt the blanket pulled up over her head. In a moment, she heard the door open, and someone enter the room.

"Here are the rest of your supper things. I'm here to take away your tea fixings," a deep male voice said. Jenna wished she could see him. She heard his footsteps halt.

"Where's Delight?" he queried. He didn't sound as thick-headed as the sisters had described. She thought there was worry in his voice. Jenna felt her throat close up.

"She's gone to bed with a fever," Jenna heard Innocence proclaim and had to smile at the youngest sister's clear attempt to sound innocent.

Jenna listened for the guard's reply.

"A fever? She might need a fever-tea."

Jenna was again surprised at the concern in the guard's voice.

"Oh no." Wonder's exclaimed in extra-sweet voice. "I think it's just too much excitement."

"Excitement?" the guard questioned. "What excitement might that be?"

Jenna could just imagine Joy glaring at Wonder for such a gaffe.

"You know, with Joy being summoned to the tower and all."

"Oh," the guard muttered. "Such goings on. Don't know what's gotten into that boy. Ye didn't go and put any funny notions in his head, did ye girl?"

Jenna realized the guard must be speaking to Joy.

"Not likely!" Joy stated in an offended tone. "He's a rude, ill-mannered clod."

Jenna thought she heard a smirk in the guard's voice as he said, "Very well, then, young mistresses, I'll see ye in the mornin'."

There was shuffling of feet and then the closing of the door with a clang and a clatter of a key being turned in a lock.

Jenna sat up suddenly to see Delight scrambling out from underneath the bed next to her, her face flushed.

"Delight, what's wrong with you?" Joy asked anxiously, walking quickly to her sister and feeling her face.

"I feel hot, my tongue's all dry, and my head aches," Delight replied.

Jenna was surprised to see Joy glare at Innocence.

Innocence smiled sweetly. "I couldn't lie, so I had to wish a fever on her."

"Oh, Braughen's Breath!" Joy muttered. "How ever did I end up with this lot of sisters?"

She turned to Jenna. "Awake, I see."

Jenna heard the sarcasm in her voice.

"Yes, I had only dozed off. Let me get out of bed so you can put Delight here."

"I'm sorry, Delight," Innocence said. "Let me bring you something to sup on."

"I'll get my night dress on and get into bed. But where will Jenna sleep?" Delight replied.

"She can share my bed," Innocence declared, smiling at Jenna. "I've room. I'm the littlest."

"No," Jenna protested. "I can sleep on the floor by the fireplace. I've done it often."

Innocence turned a wide-eyed look on Joy. "We couldn't have that, could we Joy?"

Jenna nearly laughed at Joy's disgusted frown and reply.

"Oh, stop it, Innocence. I don't care. She can sleep wherever she wants." But her voice held very little sincerity.

Wonder had been assisting Delight with her nightclothes. "Do stop arguing," she said sternly. "Let Delight get settled."

"But I won't get to hear the rest of the stories," Delight protested. "Don't say ANYTHING until the morning. I want to hear EVERYTHING."

"Yes, yes," Joy said impatiently. "You rest. Wonder can bring you something light to eat and the rest of us will have our supper."

Clearly used to obeying their eldest sister, the girls did as told. Innocence pulled Jenna over to the table and seated her next to a surly Joy.

"I'm sorry, Joy." Jenna apologized, though she didn't want to. "I didn't know they had an older sister or that they needed to ask permission to bring me inside. I just didn't..." She found her throat suddenly choked. "...didn't want to be outside alone again."

Joy stared at her with sharp, keen eyes.

I'm not pretending, Jenna wanted to say, insulted at her manner. "Besides," Jenna added, sitting up taller, "if that really was my grandmother in the dungeon, then there are things I have to find out."

"Why do you say *was*?"

Jenna frowned. "What do you mean?"

Joy replied, "Why do you say, 'If that really *was* my grandmother in the dungeon?' Why do you say *was*?"

Jenna frowned at the oldest sister. "I'm thick-headed. I don't know what you mean."

Innocence looked across the table at Jenna. "You can't be thick-headed if you can understand us when we speak a language you don't know."

"Innocence, please." Joy's voice was impatient. "I think Jenna must believe that the woman in the dungeon is no longer there."

Jenna sighed heavily. "Well, you said that was a very long time ago."

"Yes, I did. Well, I think it was. I don't really know." Joy's voice was full of frustration. "We don't really pay much attention to time here. We don't count the days. They are all pretty much the same. If we do the right things."

What does she mean by "do the right things?"

"Delight and Wonder never had a chance to finish their story. What happened in the dungeon?" Jenna asked.

"You can't tell the rest of my story," Delight shouted from across the room.

"Wonder, you're supposed to be getting Delight to sleep."

"She won't sleep, Joy. She's trying too hard to pay attention to what you are saying over there."

Joy sighed the sigh of an eldest sister. "Very well, let's move the table over there where we can all be close to Delight, and she can finish the story."

"You don't have to, Joy," Delight said, slipping out of bed. "I'm feeling better already. Innocence only wished a very little fever on me, and it's nearly gone."

Joy rolled her eyes. Jenna couldn't help but giggle.

"Think it's funny, do you?" Joy frowned at Jenna, but her look was less harsh. "You try to be in charge of these three."

Jenna smiled a sad smile. "I would love to have sisters. I had two, once."

"Once?" Delight asked softly.

"Yes, they were younger. The whole family came down with the fever when I was four. They now both lie in the church-yard."

"Oh." Innocence's one word was a volume of sympathy. She touched Jenna's arm gently and said softly, "Jenna, we can be your sisters."

"Yes, yes," Delight chimed in, sitting at the table in her night-dress, a cloak wrapped around her shoulders. "We can be your sisters."

Wonder looked as if she was about to agree but shut her mouth at Joy's frown.

Guess I can be a sister to three of the girls, Jenna thought, *but Joy is in no hurry to add me to the family.*

"Delight, I thought you wanted to tell this story," Joy said with a grunt.

"Yes, yes. I was almost done. Now, where was I?"

Innocence said, "You had told us that Genevieve had a horrid price to pay for the curse she had placed on her husband."

Delight nodded. "There isn't much more, really. We were there, standing in the dungeon, looking at her. Such a sorrowful sight. All bedraggled and beside herself with grief."

"Yes," Wonder interrupted, her face intense. "She kept saying, 'There's no one to come. No one who'll hear me call.'"

"It was then that... that we were caught." Delight shivered with the memory. "Right there in the dungeon. Where we were forbidden to go."

The three youngest sisters became still, their faces shuttered. Jenna looked at each of them in turn, wondering at their uncharacteristic withdrawal.

But Joy's face had a fierceness that took Jenna aback.

"She's there, you see," Joy said, enunciating each word carefully, in an acid-laced voice. "She's still there. I should know. I spent endless nights in the cell next to her."

Jenna could think of no reply, and the three youngest sisters remained silent until Joy rose from her chair and said, "I think we should eat our supper now."

Joy dished out their meal of piping hot stew from the fireplace kettle. Delight distributed the freshly baked biscuits the guard had brought. Wonder poured fresh tea in all the cups and Innocence added a spoonful of honey. They did all this without speaking and then ate listlessly.

The devastating tragedy of Genevieve's story had stripped the merriment from the day.

After supper, Innocence said with a weary sigh, "We are all very tired. Tomorrow, Joy can tell us all about her visit to the Boy in the Tower. It will make great entertainment at breakfast."

Joy nodded, eyeing Jenna with suspicion. "And this one will explain how she came to be here."

Delight put her arm around Jenna. "We have many stories to hear, but for now, Jenna, we'll lend you a nightdress. I think you're about the same size as Joy."

The last thing I want is to borrow something from Joy. She clearly thinks I'm to blame for the punishment she suffered, trying to rescue my grandmother.

"No, I—" she tried to protest, but her words were interrupted.

"It's in the chifforobe," Joy said with a shrug, then with the others bustled about the chamber, clearing the table, washing up dishes in a bucket by the fireplace, and banking the fire.

Before she hung her dress in the closet, Jenna made sure the small bottle was safely tucked in the pocket, then climbed into bed next to Innocence. The feeling of someone next to her a great comfort.

In spite of being physically exhausted, Jenna's mind was unable to stop whirling. Over and over, she thought through the events of the last few days—the time with Annie, Daniel and his never-ending stories, the visit to Olmigira's cave, and the journey from there to here. But where was here?

There was something in this castle that was too awful to think about. If this was a place of punishment for her grandmother's wickedness, then was she also here to be punished for something? And what of this... Keeper. She could barely say the name to herself.

Did Olmigira intend for me to find this place? Does The Keeper know I'm here? Is The Keeper the Dark Presence of my dreams? The one I must face to free Daniel?

The questions spun in her head. She looked around the room to calm herself. It was filled with a soft mellow light from the simmering fire which made comforting crackling sounds on the grate. The door was locked. She was safe here, in spite of whatever it was that roamed the castle. The soft breathing of the girls told her they were sleeping comfortably.

Her eyelids grew heavy, and she gradually drifted into slumber.

She awoke from a deep, dreamless sleep, disoriented. Some sound had aroused her.

This wasn't her loft bed. Where was she?

Someone lay next to her, breathing as one in the throes of deep sleep. The comforting heaviness of a downy blanket lay across her body. The small, flickering fire cast a soft light across the room.

Ah, the girls' chamber! Why had she awoken?

Someone had called her.

Genevieve.

That voice, pleading.

Genevieve Regina.

It wasn't a dream. The voice was clear. Distinct. And louder than she had ever heard it. As if it had come from the hallway outside.

Willing her reluctant limbs to move, she eased from beneath the comforter. The shock of the cold stone floor on her bare feet sent an involuntary gasp through her lips. She stood like a statue, her hands over her mouth. But the girls slept on, undisturbed.

Stealthily she moved across the chamber to the huge wooden door and leaned against it, listening, then heard a different sound, more disturbing than someone calling her name.

The sound of weeping.

No, weeping was too weak a word to describe the sound. It was wailing—a sound of despair so palpable that it reached out and grabbed her heart like a clenching hand.

A woman without hope.

Grandmére. Jenna said the word in her head.

The weeping suddenly stopped.

She heard me.

The guards had locked them in when they left. It was useless to try, but Jenna still pushed on the heavy oak door. Thrown off balance when the door suddenly swung open soundlessly, Jenna staggered into the dark, dank corridor.

Righting herself, she stared down the passageway, spotting a sputtering wall sconce some distance ahead near the stairway she had descended earlier. It was the only light in the eerily silent space. She was about to take a step in that direction when a voice next to her ear froze her in place.

"Don't do it. You'll be sorry."

8

TO THE SOUTH LIES FREEDOM FOR A PRICE

Jenna spun around.

"Don't go." Joy's voice was an urgent whisper.

Anger bubbled in Jenna's stomach. "I can't just leave her there," she replied in equally intense but quiet tones.

"I know you heard her weeping, but come back inside," Joy said urgently. "It's dangerous to be out here. Let's talk inside."

Jenna followed Joy back into the chamber and waited while Joy closed the hefty age-darkened door behind them.

"You heard her weeping, too, didn't you," Jenna whispered close to Joy's ear.

"Yes," Joy replied softly. "But you heard something besides the weeping."

When Jenna said nothing, Joy continued. "She called you, didn't she?" There was resignation in her voice. "She called your name. That's why you're here."

"I don't know *why* I'm here. Daniel and I were visiting Olmigira, the old woman who lives under the mountain. She said I had to go, that the Night Wind called…"

"But *she* called you before the Night Wind did."

Joy stated everything as a fact. As if she had no doubt about the answer.

Jenna nodded reluctantly. "Yes. It was her. I recognize the voice. I've been hearing it—"

"For a long time."

"Yes."

"It's my fault, you know. That you're here."

Jenna frowned in confusion. "Your fault? I don't—"

"I told her to call you."

"You knew about me?"

"No, I didn't tell her to call *you*. I just told her to call *someone*."

"*You* told her?"

"That night, when we went to the dungeon. When we heard the wailing that's like a knife in your heart."

Jenna shivered at Joy's apt description. "Yes, it is, and I can't be this close to her and not do something."

"But you can't go to her now. It's a trap." Joy took Jenna's arm. "It's cold; you're cold; come by the fire."

Reluctantly, Jenna allowed Joy to lead her to the bench by the hearth. She sat down as the oldest sister quietly stirred up the embers, creating little pockets of flame and heat and throwing a comforting warmth on Jenna's chilled body. She was even more grateful when Joy placed a woven shawl around her shoulders.

When Joy sat down beside her, Jenna continued their hushed conversation. "What do you mean it's a trap? Why would The Woman Who Wails in the Night try to trap me?"

Joy stared at Jenna intensely. "It's like that night. We also found the bedchamber unlocked. It's him. The Keeper."

"He knows I'm here?" An icy chill seeped into Jenna's soul.

"He won't harm you, as long as you obey the rules."

"What rules?" Jenna asked. "Like not going to the dungeon?"

"Yes."

"But how am I to get her out without going there?"

There was sympathy in Joy's look. "We'll talk about it in the morning. We have to think this through carefully."

Jenna wondered why Joy, who seemed like one who made careful plans, would have recklessly disobeyed The Keeper on the night Genevieve arrived. And Joy had paid for her rashness. Locked in the cell next to Genevieve. For how long? Days? A week?

That could be my fate if I am caught trying to rescue Genevieve.

Yet thinking of Genevieve locked in that dark chamber was an iron weight in Jenna's heart.

"I'm sorry," said Joy.

"What do you have to be sorry for?"

"That you're in this predicament. Away from your family and your friend... Daniel. Is that his name?"

Jenna smiled at the thought of Daniel. *What a story I will have to tell him. Better than one he could have invented.* "Yes, Daniel. He would definitely think of a plan."

"Well, dream of Daniel, and ask him to send you a plan. Let's get back to bed for now."

Jenna nodded and returned the shawl to Joy, then quietly crossed the room and crawled in beside Innocence. The warmth and comfort were enveloping.

"Goodnight, Joy," she whispered to the girl in the next bed, then whispered to the air, "Good night, Genevieve Regina."

Jenna awoke to the sound of birds and the smell of toasting bread. She felt rested and refreshed and sat up with a stretch.

"Good morning, Jenna," Delight's cheerful voice greeted her from across the room. She was holding a piece of bread over the fire with a long spit. "It's a delightful morning."

"How do you know?"

"The door is always unlocked when we awake," Delight replied, "and one of us always runs up to the courtyard to see what the day beholds. I'm not sure why. The weather's always the same. Just a very rare storm, like the one the night that, well, you know."

How can the weather be the same every day? What about winter? Or the heat of summer?

"Did you sleep well, Jenna?" Innocence said from the next bed, where she sat busily doing needlework. She must have awakened earlier and climbed out without disturbing her.

Jenna nodded.

Joy added, "She must have slept well. She snores."

Jenna nodded an acknowledgment to Joy's unspoken warning. Apparently, the other sisters had not been awakened by the wailing in the middle of the night.

"Come have some toast," Delight called.

"Let me quickly dress and brush my hair, so I'll be all set for company."

"We're having company?" Innocence exclaimed.

"No, it was just using an expression." Jenna smiled. "Don't you think you've had enough company?"

"Oh, no. I'd love company, EVERY day," Innocence proclaimed.

The girls gathered around the table and served Jenna crunchy toast with jam, bubbly porridge with cream, and hot, freshly brewed tea.

"Now tell us your story, Joy. We didn't get to hear it last night," Delight said, looking pert and recovered from her fever.

As they ate, Joy related her adventures with the Boy in the Tower.

"You remember the guard came to summon me yesterday morning, just as we were ready to go out to the grove?" Joy said.

"I was so afraid, Joy," Innocence said, a stricken look on her face. "I was sure he was going to take you to—" She stopped abruptly.

"The Keeper," Jenna finished, with just a little tremor. "But why would the guard take Joy to The Keeper?"

"At first we thought we had done something wrong... again." Innocence hung her head. "You see, after we went to the dungeon, he told us because we had disobeyed his orders, we were to be punished."

"So, he took our Joy from us," Delight continued. "He put her in a tiny little cell with no light, no windows, no visitors. Next to the Woman Who Wails in the Night.

"For how long, Joy?" Jenna asked.

Joy grunted, a look of contempt on her face. "A very long number of days."

"Yes," Innocence agreed. "It was a very long time, the most awful time of our lives and we could never, never bear it again." She looked at Jenna pointedly, as if to convey some message.

"And Joy could never, ever bear it either," Wonder added vehemently. "She came back almost wasted away to nothing. It took a long time for us to sing the joy back into her eyes."

Joy sat up stiffly. "I'd do it again if—"

"No, no!" Delight exclaimed. "You could not, and you know it. We would lose you forever the next time. He said so."

Joy explained. "They thought The Keeper had summoned me when the guard came yesterday morning, but then the guard, Guyron, said the Boy in the Tower had asked for me."

"We couldn't imagine what Joy had to endure from that boy," Wonder said, a tremble in her voice.

"There was nothing to endure except that boy's rudeness," Joy huffed.

"Go on; go on with your story," Delight urged.

"Yes, so I followed the guard across the courtyard and to the tower and then up and up and up a hundred thousand stairs."

The sisters giggled at Joy's description.

Jenna realized they all had a flair for exaggeration.

"At the top of the stairs was a landing and the door to his chamber."

Joy took a bite of toast and chewed it thoughtfully.

"What next? What next?" Wonder asked, jiggling in her seat.

"Well," Joy said with a grand gesture, "The guard unlocked the door. Imagine! The Boy in the Tower is also locked in his room! I was so surprised. I thought he was a ruler or something, but I guess he's a kind of prisoner."

Delight asked, "Did you feel bad for him?"

Joy shook her head. "I did for about one minute, until he looked at me with those cold eyes and said with a snarl, 'Come in, girl, and be quick about it. The morning air gives me a chill.' Like he was some sort of king and an old one at that!"

The younger sisters tittered.

"What did you do, Joy?" Delight prodded.

"Well, I told him my name wasn't *girl*, it was *Joy*, and that *maybe* if he got *himself* out of *this stuffy old tower* room once in a while, he'd see the *beauty of the morning* instead of feeling its chill as offensive."

"You didn't, Joy!" Wonder said with a grin.

"Oh yes, I did," Joy responded, grinning back. "He's not so much of a body to be afraid of. He's thin and wan looking, like he rarely gets any air. And he's got gangly legs and never smiles."

"Tell us about his room," Delight said eagerly.

"Ah, yes," Joy continued, "It's very tall, much taller than our chamber. And way up at the top are windows, so it gets light. Imagine living in a chamber with windows! In fact, the light looked so pretty playing in at the windows, making shadows on the wall, that I was tempted to have a dance with it, but Brat Boy wouldn't have liked it."

"Oh, Joy, you mustn't call him names," Innocence said with a shake of her head. She poured more tea for everyone.

Joy shrugged at her littlest sister's mild rebuke and went on with her story. "On one side of his chamber is a door that leads out onto the walkway that runs around the top of the tower—you know, where he watches us sometimes when we come and go from the grove. And he has manuscripts. Hundreds of them on tall shelves. And parchments and maps. And some sort of a wire contraption strung with beads. It looked like it would be fun to play with, but when I tried, he snapped at me and said it wasn't a toy; it was an abacus, a counting device."

Delight snorted her disgust. "A perfectly good toy going to waste!"

"Oh, but it would be wonderful to learn how to use it," Wonder said, her eyes wide with the excitement of something new. "I should like that very much."

"Bah!" Joy continued. "Not with Brat Boy. He asked me all sorts of questions and turned up his nose at every answer, no matter how politely I replied." She smiled her prettiest smile.

"I bet you weren't always polite," Innocence pointed out with a half-smile.

Joy rolled her eyes. "Well, penny in, penny out, as they say."

"What did he ask you?" Jenna queried, wanting Joy to stay focused on the story.

"He asked me what all of us did during the day, and then snorted when I told him we sang and danced in the grove, sometimes played in the wheat field, or sat by the stream."

Delight made a disgruntled noise.

Joy nodded in agreement with her sister's voiceless criticism. "So I asked the very same question—what did *he* do all day."

"What did he say?" Wonder asked, leaning forward.

"He said he studied, read, learned things like Latin and Greek, and mathematics," Joy replied, turning up her nose. "That he never went out to play because playing was frivolous and wasteful and just completely silly."

Jenna thought of Daniel and his "studies," and her heart winced at missing him, then asked, "Did he say why he summoned you?"

Joy frowned. "He said he has watched us from the distance and always wondered what we were about, that we always seemed so merry, and he wanted to try to understand what we laughed and sang about. I asked him if he ever sang, and he said he didn't know any songs."

Joy's sisters looked taken aback at such an unheard-of thing. No songs?

"He made me stay a very long time, sitting in the corner while he read, and then staring at me like I was one of his maps! He was so rude! We had the noon meal, and then tea, but the day went so slowly." She sighed. "But he did let me look at the manuscripts. Most of them had just words and numbers, but there were a couple with sketches which were so nice, of lovely places and even the seashore."

Joy sat quietly for a moment, as if pondering what she'd seen.

"Then he tried to teach me this game; I forget the name. He kept annoying me with all these rules about how the pieces could move. They were wonderful pieces, too. A king and a queen and knights, bishops, and horses. I wanted to make the horse run all over the table, but he got disgusted and said I wasn't playing right. I told him he didn't know how to play, and that his stupid game was no fun."

"Joy, you didn't," Innocence said with a tender smile.

"I admit, when I got ready to leave, he looked as though he was sorry I was going."

"Maybe we should all go visit him. We could teach him some songs." Innocence's face beamed with the idea.

"And he could show us that counting thing—the abacus," Wonder added, her eyes bright with anticipation.

"I could look out from the balcony to the west and maybe see the sea." Delight smiled with excitement. "How delightful!"

Delight, Innocence, and Wonder looked at Jenna, waiting to hear what she would do if she met the Boy in the Tower.

"Well, maybe he can explain how I ended up here."

Joy crossed her arms and snorted. "I don't know how the Boy in the Tower would be of any use to us. Or to Jenna. He might be spying on us and planning to report anything we said to the guards."

Concern flickered across Delight's face. "Oh, I hadn't thought of that."

"I don't think he would do anything to harm us," Innocence stated with conviction.

"Oh, Innocence, how could you know? You've never met him," Joy retorted with a sniff.

"Don't get in a huff, Joy," Wonder interrupted. "You know that Innocence has a way of sensing these things, even if she is the youngest."

Joy rolled her eyes as she made a dismissive noise in her throat. "I met him and I'm telling you, he's more of a little monster than anything."

Hating to contradict Joy as she'd warmed up a bit, Jenna said hesitantly, "Maybe he can help us with plans to rescue my grandmother."

Joy shook her head vehemently. "I wouldn't trust him."

"Joy, you know we can't help Jenna," Delight interjected, then turned to Jenna. "We couldn't stand to lose our Joy again."

Delight's words felt like a heavy cloud, and the girls finished their breakfast quietly.

As they were cleaning up, Jenna returned to the idea of meeting the Boy in the Tower. "Maybe he knows something about the routine of the guards, or the exits to the castle that I can use. But I don't plan to tell him I want to get Genevieve out of the dungeon. Joy is probably right. He might tell the guards."

Innocence suddenly clapped her hands, jumping up and down in excitement. "Why don't we invite him for tea?"

The other girls looked at her in amazement.

"Why not?" Delight said, smiling broadly. "We'll write him out a proper invitation and ask him to our afternoon tea."

"Jenna can hide beneath the bed and listen in on our conversation and maybe learn if there's a way to get her grandmother out of the dungeon," Wonder chimed in.

"But why would the Boy in the Tower want to help me?" Jenna frowned.

"He won't know he's helping you," Wonder replied. "You'll tell us the kinds of information you need, and we'll get the answers by asking sly questions."

"I think your idea is a good one, Wonder," Joy said.

"It's too bad he can't meet you, for you have the bronze key and that would raise his curiosity." Innocence pointed to the key hanging on a ribbon around Jenna's neck.

Jenna clasped the necklace given to her by the Winter Child. That encounter, just two days ago, now felt like it had happened in the distant past. "Why would The Boy in the Tower be interested in my key?" she asked.

To Jenna's surprise, the sisters began to sing a haunting, melancholy tune:

> *"To the West is the sea, wide and deep,*
>   *to the East is sunrise, awake from sleep.*
> *To the North is the magic kingdom of ice,*
>   *to the South is freedom for a price.*
>
> *A key of bronze on a ribbon hung,*
>   *opens a door where songs were once sung.*
> *To the South to the North to the East to the West,*
>   *only the bravest will stand the test."*

"You know the way to freedom?" Jenna exclaimed. "Why do you stay?"

"To the South is freedom for a price." Innocence repeated the phrase with a resigned sigh.

"What's the price?" Jenna asked.

"As we told you before," Joy said, "here we are given good things to eat. The grove and the wheat field are there to greet us every day. We have warm beds and a fireplace."

"But you are prisoners!" Jenna nearly shouted. "Don't you want to go somewhere you can be free of prison guards and dungeons?"

"Jenna," Delight said quietly, "this is our home. We'd be leaving everything we know."

"But that thing..." Jenna could barely comprehend their wish to stay anywhere near The Keeper.

"He doesn't come near us as long as we obey the rules. But if we would try to leave..." Delight stopped, shuddering.

Jenna's soul-deep dread of the Dark Presence helped her understand how frightened they'd be. "What would happen if he caught you trying to leave?" Jenna probed. "Would he lock you in the dungeon for a long time? Like he did to Joy?"

Her question was greeted by another lengthy silence. At last Wonder replied in a soft sing-song voice, a voice that wrapped itself around Jenna's mind, drawing vivid pictures.

"Somewhere hidden in a dark, unseen corner of the dungeon is another stairway that goes down and down and down, step after step after step, too many steps to count. Down into the depths of The Keeper's kingdom."

Wonder looked at Jenna with trembling lips.

"If you try to go beyond the wheat field or the grove, The Keeper will know. And The Keeper will come after you, like a specter in the night, hidden from your unseeing eyes. Before you can escape beyond the deep, dangerous forest to the South, The Keeper will drag you back to the castle. He will pull you down into the depths of the dungeon, and though you cry and scream for mercy, he will toss you down the endless stairway to the deep."

Wonder took a trembling breath, her blue eyes clouded with visions almost too horrible to put into words. "In the depths of this darkest place that exists on earth is a pit filled with the vilest of crawling things. And into this pit The Keeper will throw you and"—Wonder dropped her head and barely managed to add—"there is no way out."

"No one will ever hear your cries," Joy continued to describe the dire fate awaiting them should they try to escape. "No one will ever come to your rescue, because as he throws you into the pit, he will look into your eyes and see there all the beings, all the creatures, all the places you have ever loved."

Jenna thought of her mother and father and brothers.

"And then he will go abroad in the night," Joy continued in an unnaturally calm voice that ran shivers up Jenna's back, "into the dreams of all you have loved."

Jenna closed her eyes and saw Daniel chatting merrily.

"The Keeper will pass into the memories of those who have loved you and forever erase you from their minds," Joy continued in her flat voice. "And it will be as if you have never been, and no person, no creature, no living thing, not even the brook or the wheat field, will remember you ever were."

Innocence, who had turned whiter than the first snow in December, leaned forward and spoke softly in Jenna's ear, the anguish in her voice like the tears of a bewildered child. "And even the angels in heaven will forget you," she said in a broken-hearted whisper, her gentle mind barely able to comprehend such a thing.

For a very long time, no one spoke or moved, each wrapped within her own thoughts of such an unimaginable fate.

Jenna's mind was on her grandmother, crushed at the loss of her child. Grief-stricken, angry, bitter. Now forever locked in a dungeon, begging for someone to help her. If Jenna somehow managed to release her grandmother from the dungeon, would she herself be free to go home? To awaken Daniel from his dreamless sleep in Olmigira's cave?

But, as if reading her mind, Joy said in a fierce whisper, "Not if you are caught!"

Jenna touched her hand to the key. "Do you think this is the key to the dungeon?"

"No," Wonder said, shaking her head. "That hangs by the cell door."

"Could it be the key to her shackles?" Jenna asked.

"No, not that either," Wonder contradicted a second time. "We saw that key, a much smaller one, hanging on the post, just out of her reach. Just close enough to torment her."

"Perhaps The Boy in the Tower would know what your key opens," Innocence said.

"Yes," Delight agreed, perking up. "Let's write our invitation for the Boy in the Tower so the guards can take it to him when they come to escort us to the wheat field."

Taking parchment, an inkwell and quill pen from the shelf, Delight sat at the table as the others looked over her shoulder. In a beautiful script, she wrote: *We would be most honored to have*

Your Eminence attend us at Tea this afternoon. With humblest regards, The Sisters.

"Your Eminence!" Joy stuttered. "Oh, Delight, how can you?"

"Don't you see," Innocence defended Delight. "She's flattering him, so he'll want to come."

"Bah!" Joy muttered, pacing nearby, a stormy look on her face. But there was no more time for protest because the sound of feet in the hallway sent the girls into a panic.

"Jenna, Jenna, quickly, under the bed!" Wonder whispered furiously.

"No, No! In the chifforobe!" Joy said, pulling Jenna in that direction. "The rest of you, quickly, be busy cleaning up, or something."

Only moments after Jenna was stuffed among the clothing, she heard the hinges of the chamber door squeal as the guard swung it open, striking her with a chilling realization: last night the door swung open soundlessly.

"'Tis time to go out," the guard announced without ceremony.

Jenna heard clattering dishes.

"Sir Guyron," Innocence said, "would you be so kind as to take this note to the Boy in the Tower?"

"What! What's this about notes?"

Jenna recognized the guard's voice from the night before.

"Please, Sir Guyron," Delight said. "We'll bring you grapes from the arbor that grows near the grove." Her voice was sweet, but wheedling.

"Humpf!" Guyron replied.

Jenna wondered if that meant yes or no.

"Well, then, come now!" he ordered, but Jenna heard some kindness under his stern voice.

"Thank you!" Wonder replied.

Apparently, Guyron had accepted the note.

"Oh, I'll be right there," she heard Joy's voice near the chifforobe. "I've got to get my cloak, for I've a bit of a chill today."

"A chill, is it?" Guyron's voice came closer to the wardrobe.

Jenna held her breath, even though she was already faint for lack of air.

"Have you caught Mistress Delight's ague?"

"Her ague?" Jenna heard Joy's puzzled voice.

"Yes, yes," she heard Delight hurried answer. "That's why she was to bed so early last night, when you came back from your visit to the tower. Remember?"

"Oh, oh! Why, yes," Joy replied hastily, "I do believe I feel a bit poorly, but the fresh air will be fine and put the color back in my cheeks."

"I've no time to waste, so get the cloak and be coming," the guard replied.

Jenna felt a breath of fresh air come tumbling into the enclosed space. Hidden by the open door, Joy whispered to Jenna, "We'll try to come back early. You should be fine. Play with our games. If you are hungry, there are scones in a crock on the shelf and tea to brew." She grabbed a cloak and shut the door of the chifforobe, making sure it did not latch.

"Here I am. Sir Guyron, see, I'm ready now. Let's go, sisters, and we'll fetch the fine knight some lovely fruit."

Jenna heard the clanging door and receding footstep. She waited a long time to be sure no one returned, and then crept out of the nearly airless space, taking in deep gulps to stop the spinning in her head.

The day stretched long in front of her, and she felt like a prisoner in one of Daniel's imaginary stories. The thought of Daniel made her sadder yet. She saw him in her mind's eye, as he lay sleeping in Olmigira's cave-home.

Daniel, she called in her mind, wondering if he could hear her from this strange land she was in. *Daniel, I'll be home soon. I promise. Don't forget me.*

A doll, dressed in green, caught her eye. "Well, Little Mistress Joy," she said, "you are not so different than your bigger mistress, except you cannot make a nasty sound at the thought of the Boy in the Tower." Jenna wiled away the hours entertaining the dolls with stories of her home and brothers, and of Daniel, Annie, and the goatherd. Not knowing what the time was, she judged it by her stomach, and when she grew hungry, nibbled on a scone and drank some tea leftover from breakfast. Still tired from the last days' events, she lay back on the bed and was soon fast asleep.

Jenna wasn't sure what woke her or how long she had been sleeping, but she suddenly sensed the presence of someone in the room. Cautiously opening one eye, Jenna gave a strangled scream.

There, just inches from her face, were two eyes staring back.

9

THE BOY IN THE TOWER

Jenna rolled off the bed in the opposite direction, her heart pounding, her legs trembling.

A boy of fifteen or so, dressed in brown velvet breeches, a white chambray shirt, and a striped vest, stood on the other side of the bed glaring at her. He was thin and pale, as though he rarely saw sunshine. The thick mat of coal-black hair that fell nearly to his shoulders was the same coal-black color as his eyes. His stare was questioning and unfriendly.

Apparently, the sisters never imagined anyone would enter their chamber in their absence. Hiding her nervousness behind an affronted attitude, she demanded, "What are you doing snooping around here when the sisters are away?"

The boy's startled look told her she had taken him by surprise.

"I'm not snooping!" he said defensively. "I was invited." Uncertainty filled his eyes.

"To tea, yes, but it's not teatime," she replied, realizing who he was.

"'Tis too!" the Boy in the Tower insisted, crossing his arms defiantly.

"'Tis not!" Jenna replied, just as insistent. "If it were teatime, the girls would be here." *I really should be nicer,* she thought. *I sound like Joy.*

"Well, who are *you*?" he demanded in return, haughty once more.

Thinking Daniel would suggest a bit of imagination for this unexpected situation, she replied, "I'm their cousin, Jenna, come for a visit."

From his look of complete astonishment, Jenna might well have said, "I've just arrived here from the moon."

Putting honey into her voice, she added, "You startled me awake, young Master. I had expected my, ah, cousins, to return before your arrival so that I could be with them to offer a proper greeting."

In truth, I would have been in the closet or under a bed.

"Please forgive my poor manners." She curtsied.

The boy stared at her.

She curtsied again, waiting for his proper bow in return. Again, he only stared. Apparently, he had no manners.

Jenna sighed. "Well then, perhaps you could tell me your name, since I have done you the courtesy of telling you mine." She tried to keep the honey in her voice and the tremble out of it.

"Aidan," he said bluntly, pronouncing it I-den.

"Aidan," she repeated, giving it a bit of a lilt. "Aye, it fits you." She smiled, pleased that she knew his name. "Master Aidan, please be welcomed to our humble chamber. Here, be seated near the fireplace and I'll be about making our tea."

Jenna tried to imitate the gracious airs of Aunt Myra as she added wood to the banked coals, poured water into the cast iron tea kettle and placed it on the four-legged iron grate over the reinvigorated fire. She felt Aidan's eyes on her every step.

She placed a linen runner on the table on which she arranged the tea pot, crock of honey, and a spoon. Then, opening the thin cupboard to one side of the fireplace, she took down the tea service and placed the delicate cups and saucers at six places, arranging the chairs so all could be accommodated comfortably. From the mantle, she retrieved a small wooden box filled with biscuits and a jar of crushed tea leaves.

At that moment, the sound of girlish voices echoed down the hallway. "I'm just SO glad to be inside and soon to have tea," she heard Delight say.

It was a warning for her to hide. Stricken, she froze, clutching the box and jar and stared across the table at Aidan, unable to conceal the panic on her face.

To her stunned surprise, he stood up, took the tea things from her, and said in an urgent whisper, "Hide! Quickly!"

Jenna barely managed to make it into the wardrobe before the chamber door opened and remembered the table was laid for six. What if the guard noticed?

She heard a gasp from one of the girls and a surprised grunt from a guard.

"Master Aidan, what are ye doin' here?" The voice of Guyron filtered through the walls of the chifforobe.

"I was invited to tea," Aidan responded. Even through the press of pinafores and dresses she heard the haughtiness in his voice.

"Of course, Master Aidan. Of course, ye were. But I thought I'd be escortin' you here," Guyron said apologetically, then added, a hint of humor in his voice, "I didn't know ye was preparin' the tea as well as bein' invited to it."

"Do you think I am helpless?" She could picture Aidan glaring back at Guyron.

"No, no," Guyron muttered. Jenna thought he sounded flustered.

"Guyron, be off with you. I've come to tea, and since I was a bit early, I got the things ready so as not to be a burden on my hostesses."

"Yes, Master Aidan. I'll be back at—"

Aidan interrupted him harshly. "Guyron, I can see my own way back to the tower!" His boyish voice had a manly ring to it.

"But you know the rules, Master, about roaming the castle when—"

"Guyron, I know the rules. I shall be back in the tower before supper."

"Thank you for bringing honey cakes for our tea, Sir Guyron," she heard Innocence's lilting voice, then the shuffling of feet, and the sound of the chamber door clanging shut.

After the sound of Guyron's feet died away, Joy demanded in a fierce voice, "What did you do with her?"

Jenna burst out of her hiding place. "I'm here!"

The sisters fell upon her, talking all at once. She held up her hand. "Wait, wait," she said with a shaky laugh. "First, I must thank Aidan."

"Thank who?" Wonder asked.

Jenna walked over to Aidan. With a smile of genuine warmth and gratitude, she made a deep curtsey. "Your humble servant," she said.

Aidan reached out and took her elbow, raising her in a regal gesture. "I'm pleased I was able to be of service." He bowed in return.

"Oh, Joy," Innocence burst out, "I don't know why you called him Brat Boy! He's most wonderful! He hid our Jenna from the guards!"

Joy blushed red to the roots of her honey-blonde hair as Aidan rolled his eyes, but she muttered, "He didn't even have the manners yesterday to introduce himself by name."

The others brushed off their oldest sister's complaint in their enthusiasm to greet their visitor.

"Aidan, did you really get the tea things ready?" Delight asked, adding, "Oh, I'm Delight."

"And I'm Innocence," Innocence chimed in.

"And I'm Wonder," the last of the sisters added.

"I've seen you all from a distance, but is this really your cousin?" Aidan nodded at Jenna, who had started laying out biscuits on the plates.

Joy looked at Jenna and then at Aidan. "Oh, oh!" She doubled over in laughter. "Jenna, you're much cleverer than I thought you were!"

"Joy, don't say such things. They're hurtful," Innocence proclaimed, walking over to Jenna and flinging her arm about her shoulders.

"No, Innocence." Jenna smiled. "I am flattered that Joy thinks I'm clever."

"So, she's not your cousin." Aidan seated himself on one of the chairs. The girls followed suit, except Jenna, who poured the boiling water from the kettle into the teapot.

"We wouldn't mind if she were," Delight responded, then asked suddenly, "Why do you stare at us from the distance instead of coming to visit?"

The haughtiness returned to Aidan's face. "I was never invited before."

"Oh," Wonder replied, "I see. That does make sense."

"It was Innocence's idea to invite you to tea," Delight explained.

Aidan looked at Innocence, a small smile wrinkling the corners of his mouth.

He looks so much more handsome when he smiles, Jenna observed.

"It was very kind of you, as your sister here," he pointed his thumb at Joy, "would never have been gracious enough to do it."

"Ha!" Joy spat out. "I was commanded to come to the tower. That wasn't an invitation. And why wasn't everyone invited?"

"I thought it was easier to talk to one of you first. I couldn't find out anything about you in my books, so I knew I had to have a closer look."

"Humpf," Joy snorted. "Like we are specimens to examine."

Aidan looked at her, startled.

Joy tossed her head. "We know how to read and such. We just prefer to sing and dance and gather flowers and watch the clouds."

Jenna interrupted the exchange between Joy and Aidan to ask, "Why are you here?"

"I told you; I was invited." Aidan replied.

"No, no, I don't mean about coming to tea," Jenna explained. "I mean how did you come to live in this castle?"

He frowned in reply, his brow wrinkled. "I've always lived in the tower. As long as I can remember. I can't remember a time I didn't."

"And what do you do there?" Jenna continued her questioning.

"I study and read and learn."

"Where do you get your manuscripts?" Jenna asked.

Aidan shrugged. "They're just there. They always were."

"Don't you wonder where they came from?" Jenna prodded.

Aidan's tone flattened. "It's not good to be too curious."

"But it takes curiosity to learn," Jenna contradicted. "Is your learning limited to just things in books and manuscripts? Aren't you also curious about what's outside your tower?"

"I'm allowed to have a daily walk to observe trees and plants close up and to watch the animals in their natural habitat," he replied, a defensive note in his voice. "I walk around the battlements and outside around the perimeter of the castle. I'm allowed to witness the movement of the stars across the night sky from my balcony."

She thought that sounded like very little freedom, but then she wasn't allowed to roam freely through the fields and woods anymore. Hoping he wouldn't get angry at her persistent questioning, she asked another one. "Is there something that... keeps you here?"

Aidan's face grew shuttered. "Here I am offered manuscripts to read on natural history, philosophy, and astronomy. I have time to observe the heavenly bodies. I study the ancient languages and explore the mythology of our forebearers."

His answer reminded Jenna of the sisters' earlier responses.

"Do you know the way to freedom?" She was unable to refrain from the question that caused such pain for the sisters.

Aidan turned a shade of washed out white. "Somewhere in my tower there may be a map."

Jenna gasped. "A map!"

He turned to the sisters and with a sweeping gesture said fiercely, "Haven't they told you? There's a price!"

Cautiously, quietly, she prodded. "And what is the price for you, Aidan?"

The Boy in the Tower closed his eyes and, resting his elbows on the table, sunk his face into his hands.

"If you try to escape, The Keeper will know." His voice was anguished and low. "The Keeper will come after you, unseen like a specter in the night, hidden from your unseeing eyes. And before you can escape beyond the deep, dangerous forest to the South, The Keeper will snatch you up and drag you back to the castle into the depths of the dungeon, and though you cry and scream and flail, it will do no good. Then he will pull you, as you scream for mercy, down the endless stairway to the deep."

Aidan lifted his face and looked at Jenna, his eyes unfocused and unseeing.

"For in the depths of this darkest place in all of the earth is a pit. The Keeper will throw you into that pit where there is no light to read by, no manuscript to open, no knowledge to acquire. The days are endless and there is nothing to think about, nothing to learn."

Jenna's heart ached at Aidan's anguish, his words so similar to those of the sisters, yet reflecting the treasured possessions and pleasures they would lose.

"And he will look in your eyes and see there all the knowledge, all the learning, all the facts and figures and ideas you have gathered. And he will know of all the great discoveries and all the great discoverers, and he will go abroad at night, in the deepest of midnights, and he will creep into the mind of the writers of great manuscripts and begin to erase the knowledge they have accumulated, until there is no knowledge, no awareness, no memory. It will be as though knowledge did not ever exist, and so you cannot possibly have ever learned it. Eventually there will be nothing but a mind, starved for knowing, but nothing to know, only darkness and ignorance and emptiness."

For a long time, the room itself felt empty of knowledge; those sitting there were unable to think, imagine, or even feel. Only the crackling fireplace interrupted the silence. When Jenna finally stirred, it was once again clear that she would have to continue her journey alone.

"The tea is getting cold, we should drink it now," she said in a resigned voice.

At the distressed looks from the sisters, Jenna added, "It's all right. I know that this isn't your task. You have taken me in and already risked much. I cannot ask you to risk anymore."

She turned to Aidan. "You, too, risked much just in hiding me from the guard, even though you knew I was an outsider."

"You've come for a reason, haven't you?" Aidan asked. He looked younger now and more uncertain, not the haughty boy he tried to be.

"It appears there is, though I stumbled across this place and don't even know what or where this place is."

"You've come because of the Woman Who Wails in the Night." He said it as a fact, in the same way Joy had.

"How did you know?" Jenna was astonished.

"When she first came, I too heard the sorrowful cries. I asked Guyron who was making such a mournful noise. He said there was a woman locked in the dungeon, and that no one could do anything for her, for she had sold her soul to"—Aidan's eyes grew grim—"The Keeper."

Aidan looked at Joy. "The guards warned me not to do anything and told me that someone had tried to rescue her and was confined in the dungeon as a punishment. I thought it must have been you, for day after day you weren't with the other young singing girls when they went to and from the grove. I admit, I admired your courage."

Jenna was surprised to see Joy blush.

Innocence smiled at Aidan. "The young singing girls. Is that what you call us?"

"It's what the guards call you."

"We call you The Boy in the Tower," Delight said, smiling. "Now we know your name."

"Tell me about how you got here, Jenna," Aidan said. "Then perhaps together we can think of something to do about the situation."

The situation. He spoke so logically, so matter-of-factly. It made Jenna smile.

As they drank their cold tea and ate their biscuits, she recounted her journey, starting with the visit to Westerfordshire and Aunt Myra's story about Genevieve Regina, baby Joanna, and the sailor named Jacob who had been lost at sea. She explained how she'd been sent to Annie, the goatherd's wife, to learn the medicinal use of herbs, and that Annie directed her and her friend Daniel to pay a call on Olmigira, the old woman who lived under the mountain.

She reluctantly told them about her terrifying nightmares and how Daniel had chosen to enter one of them and that he now slept dreamlessly in Olmigira's cave. She described her mysterious encounter with the Winter Child in a frozen kingdom and how she stumbled upon Wonder, Delight, and Innocence in the grove of trees.

And finally, she told them that Olmigira said the only way she could waken Daniel was to follow the Night Wind, do the tasks that were given to her on her journey, and in the end, face the dark and evil presence that haunted her dreams.

It took a long time to tell them her tale, which they listened to without interrupting.

When she finished, Aidan said, "You have come across the North, through the Magic Kingdom of Ice. You must go South to get home."

"No, Aidan, I must go West. To the West is the sea, wide and deep. I must take The Woman Who Wails in the Night—my grandmother—to the sea. I don't know why, but I'm sure it's what I must do."

Jenna looked at each of them. "But what will happen to you after I am gone? If I can get to the dungeon and help the woman escape, The Keeper will know I have been here. I can't believe he doesn't know already."

"We will have each other," Wonder said, a look of resolution on her face. "And we have met Aidan. That means we have a new friend."

"The guards will soon be here with our dinner," Delight spoke up, concern in her voice. "Then they will lock up."

"Yes, I must go," Aidan replied. He looked at Jenna. "Tomorrow, we must find a way for Joy to sneak you to the tower so we can spend the day exploring my books and manuscripts to find something that will give us an idea how you can accomplish the task Olmigira gave you."

"How will she get to the tower without the guards seeing her?" Wonder asked.

"Perhaps I can invite a different one of you."

"And then what?" Wonder asked.

Aidan frowned. "I don't know. I'll think of something by tomorrow morning—before you go out to the wheat field. Maybe it will rain. That would make it easier if all of you are inside. Then we can work together to get Jenna to my chambers."

"I don't remember the last time it rained," Joy mused.

"We'll worry about that tomorrow," Delight said. "Now Aidan must go so he doesn't get in trouble. And we must hide Jenna, so the guards do not see her when they bring our dinner."

"Aye." Aidan stood and walked to the door, then paused. "I have been delighted to make your acquaintance and look forward to a continuance of it." He bowed formally.

The sisters and Jenna stood up and curtsied, equally as formally. "Good night, Aidan," Jenna said with a smile. The sisters echoed her words.

That night Jenna dreamt about Daniel. In her dream, they were walking along the stream by the willow tree.

"Trees are wise," he said. "Listen to what they say."

"I don't hear them speaking," she responded. "The wind is still; the trees are not whispering."

"Call the wind," he told her. "Then the willow tree will dance and sing."

She closed her eyes and called the wind. "Come, come, spirits of the wind. Come sweep upon the earth and bring the clouds. Bring the rain to refresh the earth."

In a little while, the wind began to stir, and the willow tree began to sway, its long branches rustling in the breeze.

"What does it tell you now?" Daniel said, smiling at Jenna.

Jenna smiled back. "It says the journey brings many gifts in spite of its hardships."

"Look for the gifts in the journey, Jenna," Daniel said as he turned to walk away.

"Wait, Daniel, wait for me..."

She woke up to a feel of damp chill. Innocence stirred on the other side of the bed when Jenna slipped out beneath the covers.

Innocence said in a sleepy voice. "Is it morning yet?"

"It's morning," Joy called from across the room. She was at the fireplace adding kindling and stirring up the fire. "And it's raining."

10

THE HIDDEN MAP

"Raining?" Jenna was astonished. "Then what will you do to-day?" Had the wind really listened to her in her dream? What was this strange land she was in?

"It's cold. We'll stay inside and play with our games and toys," Delight replied, flinging back the covers on her bed and throwing a shawl about her shoulders.

"That is a good thing for Aidan's plan, isn't it?" Jenna asked.

"Since we don't know Aidan's plan, who can say?" Joy said with a huff.

Jenna bit back a smile. Maybe Joy liked Aidan more than she let on. At least it seemed that Joy liked their verbal sparring.

Wonder got water boiling over the fireplace to cook porridge. "It makes a great feast on a rainy day," she explained.

"You'd better hide in the chifforobe, Jenna," Innocence said in a worried voice, halting in the process of setting the table. "The guards will be here soon."

Jenna did so, and it wasn't more than three minutes later that Jenna heard the squeal of heavy hinges and the guard named Guyron say, "Brought you cream in this pitcher for your porridge."

"Thank you, Guyron. Have you perhaps brought us an invitation as well?" Innocence said in her sweet, guileless way.

"An invitation? Whoever would invite you somewhere?" the guard answered, but Jenna thought there was an edge of discomfort to his voice.

"Why, the Boy in the Tower." Delight's voice filtered through the pinafores and aprons.

"Yes, we thought he might invite us to tea in the tower since we'd invited him to our chamber," Wonder explained.

"He might have had such a foolish idea, but I soon disabused him of the notion," the guard countered with a huff.

"So, he did invite us!" Wonder said. "Why can't we have tea with Aidan?"

'Tisn't likely the lot of you comin' to tea in the tower. Or to anything in the tower."

"But why not?" Wonder persisted.

"I don't like it. This visitin.' Don't know what's got in the boy and it isn't good. We haven't done visitin' in the past and we ain't goin' to start it now."

"But Guyron, it's a rainy day and what will we do all day?" Innocence's voice was filled with confusion.

"What you always do when it rains, of course," the guard answered.

"But I can't remember another rainy day," Innocence replied. "Do you?"

Jenna could picture the youngest sister looking at Guyron with a puzzled face.

"I'm sure it rained before. Sometime. Occupy yourself with your bits and pieces." Jenna thought Guyron sounded flustered.

Heavy footsteps and a clanging door told Jenna that he left.

When Delight opened the wardrobe door, Jenna was greeted by four gloomy faces.

"Don't worry," she said. "I'm sure Aidan will figure something out."

"Aidan's not the only one who can figure things out," Joy answered in a fierce voice. "I know how to get to the tower. I can take you there."

"Joy," Delight gasped. "You can't. It's too dangerous."

"Maybe Aidan will come for Jenna," Wonder suggested.

"No, I think we'll have a better chance at sneaking her there."

"What if the guards come and find you missing?" Delight's voice was trembling.

"They only come in the early morning to take us out to the grove and in the evening to bring dinner. They never bring us a mid-day meal."

"But we aren't usually in the chamber at mid-day meal," Wonder countered.

Jenna found it astonishing that they couldn't remember the last rainy day.

"I don't know." Joy's voice was full of frustration. "And I don't care. Come mid-day, I'm taking Jenna to the tower. So stop fussing."

Joy's sisters somberly finished breakfast preparations, and they all sat down to eat; a strained silence filled the room.

After Jenna finished her last bite of porridge, she cleared her throat.

At the sisters' expectant look, she said with a heavy sigh, "I feel like I've been such a burden to you. I'm sorry."

"Oh, no," Innocence smiled gently at Jenna. "You are not to blame. You were sent. It's clear. The Woman Who Wails in the Night, she needs you. I just wish..." She looked down, sadness on her face.

"It's alright, really," Jenna replied. "Please. I know you all would help if you could. It's much too dangerous."

"Well, let's forget about that for now." Delight jumped up. "Let's play. We can pretend to be different animals, and the others must guess what we are."

"Oh yes, that sound like a merry time," Wonder agreed. "Come everyone! Let's clear away breakfast quickly so we can play Delight's game."

Thus, Jenna and the girls wiled away the time, playing and laughing. But all the laughter dissipated several hours later when Joy suddenly said, "Well, now, we've had some merriment, but it's time for me to show Jenna the way to the tower."

Her declaration was greeted with worried looks.

"If the guards happen by, tell them I had to return a game piece to the Boy in the Tower."

"What game piece?" Delight asked.

Joy reached into her pinafore pocket and held out a small tower carved from ivory.

"Oh, Joy, you didn't."

Joy grinned. "It was so dear, and I thought it would be so much fun to have on our shelf."

At Innocence's frown, Joy added, "Well, he has three more of them."

"Maybe he needed all four to play the game," Wonder said with a shake of her head. "You are very bad, Joy."

Joy grimaced. "Well, now I must return it because I've had a twinge of conscience. You won't be lying if you say that's what I've done. But I think the guards will not bother us at all. This rainy day has everyone unsettled."

"Will they be out in the courtyard or on the watch towers if it's raining?" Delight asked.

Joy shrugged. "Who can say. Maybe they still have to be guarding whatever it is they guard. No matter. Come now, Jenna. We've a long way to go, and we need to be quick but silent. Can you be silent?" Joy frowned at Jenna.

Jenna tried to keep the irritation out of her voice. "Yes, I can. I often walk with soft steps in the woods and have sat so quietly the birds and squirrels and deer come near."

"Very well." Joy sounded unconvinced. "The way is not difficult."

"If it's not difficult, perhaps I should go alone," Jenna suggested, hesitantly.

"No," Joy contradicted with an edge to her voice. "I must talk to Aidan about a plan to get you back safely to our chamber. So come, let's not delay any longer."

Jenna envied Joy's matter of fact manner. She herself dreaded leaving the safety of the sisters' chamber. Oddly enough, since arriving, she had not once had a terrifying nightmare in which the Dark Presence crept up on her, its rattling breath near her ear. Although she sensed it was somewhere in the castle, it seemed to be keeping its distance. But she worried that if she went wandering around the castle that could change in an instant.

Joy gave her little time for such thoughts, however, because she grabbed her hand and pulled her to the chamber door.

"Remember, we must be as silent as mice, as we have to walk past the kitchen. When I went to visit Aidan, there were people there preparing meals."

With a quick glance at the other sisters, Jenna followed Joy down the passageway. Candles burning in widely spaced sconces cast more shadows than light. In a moment, they passed the stairs where she had hidden on her first day and turned left down the long hall leading to the southeast tower.

Soon came the savory odor of frying onions and the echoing voices of men in conversation. As they approached an open doorway on the left, Joy signaled her to stop. Jenna watched, her throat constricted, as Joy moved close enough to peek around the corner, then gestured for Jenna to run across the opening. Jenna scurried softly to the other side, not daring to glance in, halting breathlessly as she looked back at the oldest sister.

Voices! Some leaving the kitchen approaching the doorway!

"Where do you think you are going, Guyron?" A voice unknown to Jenna asked.

"To take this lunch tray to the girls," Guyron responded.

"Since when have we given the girls lunch? It's breakfast and dinner we give them," the other man said.

"Aye. But 'tis a rainy day."

"What does that have to do with anything? Why would we do things differently?"

"How am I to know? When is the last time we had a rainy day?" There was more alarm than uncertainty in Guyron's voice.

"Well, seein' as how it's already fixed, you may as well take it to them. But wait, Guyron, you forgot the bread."

Jenna heard the shuffle of feet retreating from the door. She looked with panic at Joy.

With accompanying hand gestures, Joy mouthed the words, "You go. I must go back."

Jenna, her heart pounding, nodded her understanding. She watched Joy spin on her heels and speed silently down the hall. Jenna did the same, in the opposite direction, constantly peering over her shoulder to watch for Guyron. By the time he came out of the kitchen, she was far enough down the passageway to press herself against the wall in a shadowed area.

Guyron never looked her way as he lumbered toward the girls' chamber.

Grateful, Jenna turned and raced ahead through the damp, dim corridor. It seemed to take forever to reach the next set of circular stairs. Once there, Jenna peered up the curved stairway. She would have no place to hide if she encountered anyone coming down.

Taking a deep breath and lifting her shirt in one hand, she hurried up the steps, hugging the inner wall, the light growing brighter as she ascended. After several winding turns, she was at the ground floor landing. Across from her, a massive iron-hinged wooden door stood open to the courtyard. A steady drenching rain filled the day with gloom.

After a quick glance down the hallway to her left, she headed up the next flight of stairs. Narrow slits in the stonework let in gray light and cold rain. Jenna shivered. Round and round she mounted, treading carefully, for the stairs were damp and slick. In moments, she reached the second story landing.

His chamber is at the top of the tower, Jenna reminded herself. *And this isn't the top. There's more stairs.*

Just as she was about to continue her climb, she heard a noise on the steps above her. Panicked, she ran into the passageway and squeezed herself into the area behind the stairwell. She held her breath as stealthy steps descended the staircase.

Who is it that's walking so quietly? A guard wouldn't care if he was heard.

She gave into her suspicion and peered around the corner just as Aidan began to descend the stairs to the main floor. Jenna raced to the stairwell and called his name in a loud whisper.

Aidan spun around, one foot on the step below to keep from falling.

"Jenna! For the love of—You frightened the wits out of me. Come, quickly. Up to my chamber."

He raced past Jenna and back up the stairs.

Jenna scurried after him. At the top landing, she darted into the chamber as he held an arched wooden door open. He quickly closed it behind them.

She stood still a moment to catch her breath and calm her heart.

"Did you come alone?" Aidan asked.

Jenna shook her head no but held out her hand as Aidan made a sudden move for the door.

"No," she said, waving her hand. "We started out together. Joy was leading me. But the passageway goes by a kitchen, and we heard Guyron and another man talking about taking a tray to the girls. She had to go back so there'd be no suspicion."

Aidan nodded. "She made a wise decision. For being so hot-headed, it's almost a surprise."

Jenna smiled in amusement. "I think the two of you like to fight."

Aidan raised a haughty eyebrow. "It's her. Always finding something to argue about."

Jenna laughed. "Well, it's not as if they are one-sided argu-ments. You could ignore her."

"Ignore her? Joy? I think that would be impossible." Aidan shrugged his shoulders.

Jenna nodded in agreement. "She can be forceful."

She looked around at the large, circular room. It was the entire top of the tower and just as Joy had described. The bound manuscripts were everywhere—huge shelves reaching to the ceiling, with a ladder on wheels. She had never seen so many books.

It's a wonderful room, and it fits him, she thought. Maps were spread out on a huge wooden table, and tapestries of battles and warrior knights hung on the walls. One area of the room was filled by a huge four-poster bed surrounded by thick red, velvet curtains. It looked like a place a king would sleep.

"Your chamber is nice."

"It's a room. I don't think much about it," Aidan responded, indifferently.

"But it must be lovely to study here. I know Daniel would like it very much."

"Daniel. Your friend." Jenna detected an odd note in Aidan's voice.

"Yes, my friend."

"I don't have... friends." His voice was soft, almost puzzled.

"Maybe not before, but you have some now," Jenna inter-jected, smiling at him.

Aidan's face was a study in confusion. "Yes, I guess so. I suppose I am friends with you and the sisters. So, it isn't just me in the castle any longer."

"There never has been just you, Aidan," Jenna contradicted gently. "The sisters have been there all along. You know that."

"Yes, but I just never thought about talking with them. Or that we could be friends. No one ever said I could. Or should. But then I found something that made me begin to wonder."

Jenna heard a worried tone in his voice and prodded carefully. "It worries you, doesn't it, Aidan? To be curious about anything other than your studies."

"Well, yes. I told you what the cost is if The Keeper catches us trying to escape."

"But you're not escaping, Aidan. You're just reading what's on your shelf."

Aidan's face was deeply troubled. "Yes, but somehow, I know it's not good to be too curious. Gets you in trouble."

"But look where your curiosity has gotten you. You've met Joy, Innocence, Wonder and Delight. Isn't that a good thing?"

Aidan nodded. "Yes. It is. But something seems to be changing. I'm not sure why."

Jenna watched as Aidan sat lost in thought, realizing she could have easily answered his question. It was her presence in the castle that had caused a disruption.

Aidan sighed. "Well, no sense in racking my brains about it. Let me show you what I found—but wait!" He smacked himself on the head. "Such a host. I didn't offer you any refreshment."

Jenna giggled.

"What's so funny?" Aidan knotted his eyebrows together.

"The girls would think it's amusing that you would offer refreshment."

"I have learned the manners of a good host." Aidan held himself upright. "It's just that Joy set me on edge right away, and I forgot to use them."

He said it in such a chagrined way that Jenna nearly hooted with laughter.

"Oh, Aidan, I'm sorry. I can quite understand. Joy could certainly make anyone forget their manners when she puts on her haughty airs." She grinned at him.

Aidan returned her smile. "Oh well, perhaps I can make it up to her someday. Come to table. Have some tea. The kettle's been warming all morning. Guyron brought some cold mutton for lunch when he brought up my breakfast. Let's eat."

As Jenna and Aidan ate lunch, Aidan told her about his routine and studies. In return, she told him about her home and family. He asked a lot of questions about Daniel, and as she told him more about her friend, a twinge of loss gnawed at her heart. In many ways, Aidan reminded her of Daniel, especially his interest in so many things.

Jenna found herself warming to this boy who lived in a tower. *He's got a sarcastic edge, a bit like Joy,* she thought, then almost chuckled out loud thinking of how Joy would react to such an idea.

"Come, let me show you what I found the other day," Aidan said as they finished their tea. "I was looking among some of the manuscripts on the upper shelves. Ones I don't recall looking at before." He had a puzzled look on his face. "I don't even know why I was doing that."

"Don't you use all your books and manuscripts?" Jenna asked, though she couldn't imagine how he possibly could.

"Usually only ones in the lower areas."

Aidan climbed the iron ladder to a top shelf. "Where'd I put it? I tried to put it back so it wouldn't be obvious that I had found it." He glanced down at Jenna. "I don't know why," he answered her unspoken question. "I felt nervous for even looking here. Ah, found it!"

He climbed back down and handed Jenna a small, leather-bound manuscript, then cleared space on the large table near the fireplace by rolling up maps and moving a stack of books. They sat next to each other and Aidan opened the manuscript, turning the beautifully lettered but yellowed pages, some decorated with vividly colored, hand-painted illustrations.

"It seems very old," Jenna said softly.

"It's full of stories of long ago," Aidan said, "About how a land was conquered and a kingdom established. Of the family that ruled the kingdom at that time." He sighed deeply. "It makes me think, I'm not sure why, that there is something odd about this place I live."

Jenna wanted to shout, "*What's odd is no one else finds it odd!*"

"I don't know," he continued hesitantly, "you talk about your mother and father and brothers. I have no memory of parents or siblings or even my childhood."

Jenna shook her head, trying to understand. "How can that be, Aidan? You're fifteen, sixteen? How can you not remember your mother and father? Are you an orphan?"

"I don't know. I never even thought about it before the other day. Some things I remember, but others I seem to forget. Even if something strange happens, something out of the ordinary, like a rainy day, I have trouble remembering it the next day. You'd think something unusual would be memorable."

He frowned in concentration. "I woke up this morning, and I did what I usually do every morning. It wasn't until Guyron came with my breakfast and said, 'Master Aidan, 'tis raining. You shall need your cloak later this morning for your walk about the battlements,' that I even remembered I was to invite the sisters to tea."

Jenna saw something deeper than confusion in Aidan's eyes.

"Jenna, I know this will sound impossible. But until Guyron mentioned the rain..." He said the words slowly, as if struggling to get them out. "I... I... didn't even think about you or the sisters. It was as if... as if I had forgotten about yesterday. Almost as if it hadn't happened."

He dropped his head into his hands. "I used to think that we'd only be punished if we tried to escape." His voice was low.

Jenna leaned forward to hear him.

"But it's not just then. It's always. I think we are being punished all the time—in a way I've never realized before."

Jenna felt Aidan's bewildered sadness.

"Every day we are robbed of our memories," he muttered, an edge of anger creeping into his voice.

Jenna tried to comprehend what he meant. "But Aidan, you all remembered the Woman Who Wails in the Night. And you remembered the girls. You invited Joy to tea. You came to visit."

"Yes. But there are constant reminders about those things. Who could forget the Woman Who Wails in the Night when you hear her crying?" He shivered. "Sometimes I can still hear her. It is almost unbearable so that I have to cover my ears. And the girls. I see them every morning leaving the castle. It's just that once I am reminded, then I remember everything. Once something opens a door to memory, it comes back. But there seem to be large parts of my past that I can't remember. I must have had a mother and a father."

Jenna's heart ached for Aidan's unanswerable questions. *He's not going to be satisfied with only his books and his tower anymore. He will want answers that his books can't give him.*

She somehow had created a disruption by entering the castle. Was it something she should feel guilty about or that he would regret?

"Aidan, I have many unanswered questions as well. When I left Olmigira's cave, it was mid-summer night. As I walked through the woods, it turned to winter. That makes no sense. And then when I found the girls in the grove, it was spring."

Aidan nodded. "We always have spring. That really isn't natural, I think. I've read about the seasons. But here they seem to be almost halted." He sighed a deep, shivering sigh. "I haven't thought about any of this before. Why is that?"

Jenna gently touched Aidan's arm. "Aidan, my grandmother died before I was born. How could she be here as a young woman? How could I be here? And who is The Keeper?"

Aidan shrugged his shoulders. "I don't know. It hurts my head to think of it. It isn't logical. Things should be logical. But look in this manuscript. See the drawing? It's a design for a castle. I studied this long and hard, and I think it is this castle."

Jenna looked as he pointed out the features.

"I memorized the drawing and then walked out on the battlements the day before I invited Joy to visit. The drawings seem to match the castle's design. And look, here, there is a door to the West, a door that leads to a path to the sea. But see, here." Aidan pointed to a note on the drawing. "It says it was shut and locked a very long time ago. And the key stolen."

Aidan looked up at Jenna, his face grim. "It says here, below the map of the castle, that it was a bronze key."

Jenna's stomach did a somersault.

"And..." Aidan pushed the manuscript over to Jenna. "See, there, what it says."

Jenna pulled the manuscript in front of her and stared down at the words on the page.

But a future day awaits, fear not. A courageous maiden will undo this knot. In the hands of a maiden, young and pure, will a key of bronze unlock a door.

"You have a bronze key," Aidan said. "You said that girl... what did you call her—The Winter Child—gave it to you."

Aidan reached over and turned the page. "Look. Here is a map of the land around the castle and here"—he traced his finger along the map—"is a path that leads from the western wall down to the sea. It indicates marshes and boggy areas and right there is a warning not to stray from the path or your life may be lost."

Jenna leaned back in the chair, her mind swimming. "Aidan, I don't know why, but I know if I get Genevieve out of the dungeon, I need to take her to the sea. I could do that by using that door and that path. The Winter Child said I would know how to use the key when the time came. The bronze key must open that door! But how am I to get to the dungeon?"

She felt a cold fear creeping through her veins.

"I think there is a way to get there besides through lower passageways of the castle," Aidan said and turned back to the diagram. "Look. The western door is across from a stairwell that leads into the dungeon. We could go in the western door using your key and enter it that way."

Jenna turned to stare at Aidan. "We? Aidan, you can't. You know what happened to Joy. How she was locked away for all that time."

Aidan's face took on a fierce look, one that reminded her of Joy. "There are things that I have to know. And I can't stay up here in this tower day after day. Not anymore."

"Whether you help me or not, I don't think I should delay much longer," she said. "The Keeper must know I am here. The sooner I get my grandmother—if that's truly who she is—away from here, the better it will be for you and the sisters."

But what would she do when she got her grandmother to the western sea? There would be no escape with their backs to the sea. Her mind swirled. *And what about getting home? Back to Daniel in Olmigira's cave. To my mother and father and brothers?*

Aidan's voice caught her attention. "You are quite right. I think that today is the day to carry out the plan."

"Today?" Jenna stood up, alarmed. Yes, she wanted to be quick about it, but today?

"Yes, today, because everyone is all aflutter with the change brought on by the rain. Though why should rain be a strange occurrence?" He seemed to ask the question to himself.

"I... I don't know. How could I just leave without saying goodbye to the girls." She tried to hold onto a calmness that was rapidly slipping away. Things were being decided too quickly.

"Wait. I've more to show you," Aidan said, gesturing for her to sit down again. "Here, further back in the book it says something really odd." He began to read. "And the flame will dance, and near the dancing flame no vile or evil may approach."

Jenna shook her head. "A dancing flame? What could that mean?"

Aidan continued reading. "And though the flame will dance and burn, the sea-green bottle will not grow warm, but stay cool to the touch, as cool as the bubbling brook."

Jenna's eyes widened. "A sea-green bottle?" She stared at Aidan, her heart constricting. "I have such bottle. I found it on the beach at Westerfordshire."

"What does the bottle look like? How big is it?"

"It's not big at all. Just fits into my hand. And it did the strangest thing when I walked through the woods after leaving the Winter Child—it glowed."

Aidan leapt up from the table with a whoop. "That's it. We could fill the bottle with oil, and I could cut a thin piece of hemp from the rug and use it as a wick. That must be it. Where is the bottle?"

"It's in the chifforobe in the girls' chamber."

"We must retrieve it and get your grandmother from the dungeon before the guards lock up for the night."

Jenna struggled to get her breath at Aidan's headlong rush into action. "But the girls didn't go out into the meadow. Did the guards even open the front gate and lower the drawbridge?"

"Yes," Aidan said. "On my walk, I saw that they had done so. In spite of everyone being all out of sorts about the rain, they still opened the gate."

Jenna looked at Aidan, trying to stay focused, her mind whirling with what might lie ahead.

"And it will soon be tea," Aidan said, standing and in an urgent voice continued, "We need to sneak down to the girls' chamber now and get back here before dinner hour. That will give us an hour to get outside the castle and re-enter by the Western gate before the gates are locked at first watch."

Jenna struggled to keep dizziness and disorientation from overcoming her.

"Let's go now!" Aidan commanded, grabbing her hand and hauled her to her feet.

Please. No! I don't want to! I don't want to go anywhere near that unspeakable thing.

But Aidan didn't hear her silent plea and pulled her toward the chamber door.

II

THE BRONZE KEY

The castle was eerily quiet as they hurried to the sisters' chamber. They neither saw nor heard anyone in the passageways or the kitchen. When they approached the chamber, Aidan told Jenna to hide beneath the stairway until he was sure there were no guards with the girls.

In a moment he was back, whispering, "It's clear to come. Hurry."

Jenna scampered after Aidan through the open door of the sisters' chamber. As he was closing the door, the four sisters fell on her with exclamations and embraces.

It's like I belong to them. Is this what it's like to have sisters?

"Oh Jenna," Innocence said. "We missed you so. It was such a long day without you to talk and sing with." Wonder and Delight echoed Innocence's sentiments, but Joy was coldly calm as she said, "I am relieved that you are safe."

Jenna and Aidan joined the girls at the table, and Jenna told them about their discoveries in Aidan's manuscript and the reference to the bronze key and the door in the western wall, her mind oddly disconnected from her words. As if she were watching herself and not actually experiencing the moment.

"What does all this mean, Jenna?" Wonder asked, concern lacing her words.

Aidan, who had been quiet during Jenna's explanations, spoke up. "It means that today, before first watch, Jenna must find her way into the dungeon and rescue the Woman Who Wails in the Night. To do that, she and I must find the entrance to the castle from outside the western wall and use her bronze key to open it."

"What? What's this *she and I*," Joy demanded suddenly. "And don't speak of this task as if it were a story in a book."

Aidan face flushed slightly, but he rolled his eyes. "Don't be difficult."

"Me difficult? Who is the difficult one here?" Joy countered, glaring back at him.

"Stop," Innocence said softly. "We mustn't argue. We've no time. Joy, you must listen."

Joy folded her arms. "Very well. I'll listen... for now."

"Won't the door in the western wall be hard to find?" Wonder asked. "If it hasn't been used in many years it might be overgrown with vines and vegetation."

Aidan nodded. "That could be true. You've a sharp mind."

"Of course, she has a sharp mind. Do you think we are idiots?"

"Joy," Wonder interjected. "Don't be so snappy."

Joy made a face.

"Go on, Aidan," Wonder urged him.

"Once we've reached the stairwell that leads into the dungeon. From there..." Aidan stopped, his voice beginning to waver. "I... we..."

Jenna had been watching their exchange, trying to overcome a sense of being an indifferent observer. They were describing what she was going to be doing, and it sounded like a fairytale. She broke in. "From there it is *I*, not *we*, Aidan. You know the consequences of being caught."

She closed her eyes, taking deep breaths, trying to shut out the confusion that was threatening to overtake her mind. "Aidan, I think you are taking too great a risk to go with me even as far as the western door. I need to go alone," she said as she opened her eyes.

"Oh, no," Delight said, horror in her voice, as she grasped Jenna's hand. "You must let Aidan escort you. He is willing, and he is brave."

Aidan's pale face flushed pink. "I wish I were brave," he replied, his voice suddenly fierce. "Then I would go into the dungeon with her. I would help unshackle the Woman Who Wails in the Night. I would go with her to the western sea. And I would face that vile..." With an indrawn breath, he stared down at his tightly clenched hands.

Jenna tried to wrap herself in a blanket of calm. To breathe evenly. *It's just one thing first. And then the next. Don't think too many steps ahead.*

She turned to Aidan and said, "It isn't your duty to do that, Aidan. Or for any of you to help. I know you want to, but it's my task. Genevieve called me. In the dreams. After I responded to her call, it was then the Dark Presence appeared."

Her skin grew clammy as those appearances came to mind, but she continued to speak.

"It's as if he was trying to frighten me away. To keep me from responding to the call. But here I am. I don't really understand how I actually got here and sometimes I think this is a dream, but looking at each of you, I can't imagine that something so real could be a figment of my imagination."

She took a deep breath. "I didn't know where I would end up when I followed the Night Wind. I knew I had to free Daniel from his endless sleep, and I could only do that if I stood face-to-face with the Dark Presence. I didn't realize I would also need to free my grandmother from her prison cell."

As tiny tremors shook her body, she felt the warmth of an arm across her shoulders.

"You have the heart to do it, Jenna."

Jenna turned to see Joy's face close to hers, her eyes intense and piercing. "It's the heart that gives courage. It doesn't mean you won't be afraid. It's wise to be afraid at times. Courage and impulsiveness are not the same thing."

Joy's words were a balm, soothing her mind. Fear had been her companion for so long. *Maybe fear is a friend, after all.*

"You would have never left Olmigira's cave if you didn't have the heart for this journey," Joy insisted. "Your heart tells you what the right thing is to do. You know it is the right thing; you follow your heart, and you do it. That's what courage is."

Aidan's deep sigh caught all of their attention.

"Joy is right, you know," he said quietly. "You have to know when to act and when to wait. I can hardly think that this is a time for me to wait. Yet, if I interfere with Jenna's task, I might cause more harm than good. Nor must you unduly interfere, Joy."

Joy nodded, reluctantly consenting.

There was relief on Delight's face at Joy's unspoken promise.

Jenna looked around the table. Her heart ached to think she would be leaving them so soon. This very night. The intensity of her connection to these four girls in so short a time astounded her. *Time seems to be irrelevant in this place.*

"We must go now, Jenna." Aidan's words were soft but urgent.

Innocence and Wonder retrieved Jenna's apron from the chifforobe and helped her put it on. "Here, Jenna, take your cloak. It will be cold outside the castle at night," Delight said.

Jenna made sure the green bottle was secure in her pocket and that the bronze key still hung safely around her neck.

Aidan looked at each of the sisters in turn. "You must stay here, and spend the night as you usually do, so there is no suspicion."

The girls nodded in assent and gathered around Jenna in a circle, joining hands. Delight began to sing a soft, gentle melody.

Farewell my treasured one, adieu. The distant lands are calling you. They sing of songs and faces dear. Go home in peace, and do not fear.

Jenna pictured her parents and brothers sitting at the table in their cottage, Daniel laughing as he entertained them with his stories. That vision gave her the strength to say her goodbyes without collapsing in tears, though she struggled to say the words.

"Goodbye, blessings upon you." Her lips trembled as she gave each sister a tender kiss on the cheek.

"Take care of our Jenna, Aidan," Innocence said suddenly, hugging him fiercely.

Aidan nodded, taking in a deep, trembling breath, then standing stiffly upright, took Jenna gently by the elbow and led her out the chamber door.

With a quick backward glance at four sisters who stood clutching each other, staring after her with stricken faces, Jenna followed quickly behind Aidan. Once they reached the passageway, Aidan took Jenna's hand firmly in his and whispered, "Hurry." They walked swiftly, keeping along the wall, stopping frequently to listen and confirm it was safe.

With each step, her fear increased. Would they be discovered by the Dark Presence?

When they finally neared the landing below Aidan's tower room, he pointed to the nearest door in the passageway, then mouthed the words, "Be very quiet—the guards."

Jenna heard men's laughter and the clink of dishes and pans. *They must be eating dinner*, she thought, homesick for a meal with her family. With swift feet, she and Aidan rounded the wall and soundlessly mounted the final flight of stairs to Aidan's tower room.

Once inside, Jenna collapsed on the nearest bench, quavering. Aidan sat down heavily beside her, leaning against the stone wall. After a few moments of rest, Jenna stood up. "I'm ready, now."

Aidan retrieved the manuscript from beneath his bed where he had hidden it. Opening it to the map, he ripped the page from the book and folded it into a small square.

"Put it in your pocket," he said to Jenna, then returned the manuscript to the upper shelf where he had found it.

"It won't be long till the guards bring dinner. You must hide on the bed. The curtains will keep you from view." He pulled aside the thick, plush curtains, and she clamored up the footstool to reach the high mattress.

In spite of the sense of urgency, Jenna giggled.

"What do you laugh at?" Aidan said, frowning.

"I feel like I'm playing hide and seek with little Peter."

A small smile flickered on Aidan's face. "I'm glad you can laugh. My heart feels like stone."

"Oh, Aidan, I've put you all in danger."

"No, we were in danger of forever falling into this half-dreaming awareness we have been existing in. But no time for philosophy. Sit very still so the bed curtains don't move." He drew them closed.

As the area around her plunged into darkness, Jenna lay down on the soft, luxurious bedspread. Pinpricks of light penetrated tiny worn spots in the draperies. She felt lightheaded and illogically giddy. In a few moments, the grinding of iron hinges announced the guards' arrival.

"Master Aidan," the voice of Guyron came clearly across the room. "We've brought your evenin' repast. I hope the day's studyin' has been profitable."

Jenna had to clamp her hands over her mouth to keep from giggling. If only the guard knew. A sudden thought vanquished her unsteadiness: *I wonder if the guards are under the control of The Keeper.*

Sounds of shuffling feet and clinking dishes were followed by Guyron's voice. "We'll be back in an hour to retrieve the tray and to lock up."

"Aye, Guyron." Aidan's voice was calm, indifferent.

Probably the way he always talks to the guards, she thought. A moment after the thump of feet and the clunk of the door closing, the bed curtain was flung open.

"We've got to eat quickly; there's only a bit of time."

Jenna's stomach felt like the ocean on a stormy day. "I'm not hungry; I couldn't eat."

"You must. You'll need strength for what you must face."

Jenna sighed. "A bite or two."

She joined Aidan at the table and took a spoonful of the thick, rich stew. She almost gagged. "No, I can't Aidan. I'm sorry. Maybe the bread."

While she chewed slowly on the freshly baked bread, its rich yeasty aroma like a perfume, Aidan wolfed down the stew.

How like a boy. No matter what the situation, they can always eat.

"I'm not hungry either," he said between mouthfuls, "but I don't want them to be suspicious if the food hasn't been touched. Put the rest of the bread in your pocket. You'll be hungry for it later."

Aidan retrieved his cloak from a hook near the door and flung it around his shoulders.

"We must go back two flights of steps, past the landing near the guards' room and down to the courtyard. Then we must go across the courtyard, out the drawbridge, and around the castle to the western side. It's growing dark. It will soon be first watch."

Aidan took a step toward the door, then stopped. "No, wait."

Jenna looked at him expectantly.

"There's something I just remembered—your small bottle."

Jenna reached into the pocket of her pinafore and retrieved the small bottle.

"Here, give it to me!" He said in the authoritarian voice that Joy so resented. Aidan softened his manner, explaining, "The dancing flame."

Jenna carefully handed him her treasure from the sea. He took it to the table and retrieved a small vial from the cupboard.

"It's walnut oil. Very precious." He poured some into her bottle. Then he took a knife from the table and cut a length of cord from the underside of the rug, placing it in the bottle to make a wick. Using a long thin sliver of wood, he lit the wick.

In a moment, a flame appeared, no taller than the finger on a baby's hand. As Jenna watched, the flame grew stronger, more intense, deepening in color to a rich yellow, nearly the color of gold. Then it began to move from side to side, around the edge of the bottle's opening, as if it were...

"Dancing," Jenna said, struck with the flame's gentle grace. She slipped her hand around the base of what had become a lantern and found it as cool as a mountain stream.

"Now we're ready," Aidan said with conviction, then smiled one of his rare smiles.

Do the next right thing, and you'll be fine, she told herself.

As they slipped out the door and down the stairs, Jenna held the treasured bottle in her hand. The flame burned steady and bright, casting a warm, comforting glow in front of them. Jenna thought it odd that they could move about the castle like this and encounter no one.

Reaching the ground floor, Aidan led the way through an arched opening into the courtyard. He pointed to the opening on the far side of the courtyard that led out to the drawbridge.

"We'll stay close to the wall, under the cloister walk, so we aren't spotted. Sometimes the guards stand on the battlements across the way." His voice was hushed.

The day was growing dimmer, and Jenna heard a rumble of thunder in the distance. The air had grown much colder; she was grateful for her cloak. Jenna took a step to her left, the shortest route to the drawbridge, but Aidan held her back.

"This way," he whispered, pulling her arm gently to the right. "Less chance of running into someone."

Jenna nodded and followed. Urged on by the approaching storm, they hurried along the interior walls surrounding the courtyard.

The castle had a deserted air. No evening songbirds bid the sun goodnight. The winds picked up the dust in the courtyard and made small swirling eddies. They passed a barred passageway and boarded-over arched windows with shards of broken glass between the slats of wood. This part of the castle seemed abandoned.

She stopped. There was something about this doorway.

"What's wrong?" Aidan whispered, alarmed.

"This place," Jenna said softly, "what is this place?"

"I'm not sure. I think it might have been the chapel at one time."

"This is where it is," Jenna said, with excitement in her voice.

"Where what is?" Aidan's voice was edged with impatience and nervousness. "We've got to go. The entry is on the western wall of the castle."

"Isn't this the western wall?" Jenna asked.

"Yes, yes, it is, but hurry, we've got to go the whole way around the courtyard, out the drawbridge, and around the castle to reach this wall on the outside. *That* is where the door is."

His hurried, rushed whisper revealed the fear he was trying to hide.

Jenna touched his shoulder. "From the drawings of your castle, wasn't the chapel above the dungeon? Couldn't there be a way to reach the dungeon through the chapel?"

Awareness dawned on his face. "Yes, yes, you're right. And it would make sense then that The Keeper would close off the entry to the chapel to limit access to the dungeon."

"Yes," Jenna replied. "We don't have to go outside; we can get in this way. Help me pull back the boards."

Many of the boards barring the archway had rotted with age. With little effort, they opened a space wide enough to squeeze through and stood in a narrow space between the boards and the chapel door. But the door didn't budge.

"Let's use our shoulders. Shove it together," Aidan said softly and with a nod to Jenna, they flung themselves against the huge wooden door. With a creak of rusty hinges that echoed like a cannon shot across the courtyard, the door swung open, tumbling them into a dark, empty space.

Jenna froze, waiting for guards to come running. Aidan stood nearby, poised for danger. When no shouts or pounding feet came their way, Aidan signaled her to step forward. The dancing flame cast a soft, gentle glow into the deserted chapel revealing stone pillars reaching into the gloom above.

It's musty and in disrepair, but it's still beautiful.

Aidan said, his voice full of awe, "The floor plans of the castle show there was a chapel, but I never thought..."

Jenna sensed the echoes of long-ago chants, musical prayers that had long since vanished into the damp, chill, soaring space of the chapel, lingering still for those who could hear.

The squeal of hinges sent Jenna spinning around. She turned in time to see Aidan disappear through a small door.

"Here," he called to her. "A hallway."

Jenna caught up to him as he was turning the corner into another hallway that ended abruptly at a walled-off archway.

He turned to face her as he put his right hand on a door. "This is the western wall and here's a door! Give me your key!" In his excitement he forgot to whisper.

With shaking hands, Jenna put the dancing flame on the floor in front of her and carefully pulled the red ribbon with its bronze key up over her head and held it out to Aidan.

He snatched it from her hand, then thrust it into the keyhole, attempting to unlock the door. But no matter how he tried, the key would not turn. Muttering under his breath, he pulled the key out of the lock and stepped back, glaring at the door as if it were an enemy and then at the key in his hand as if it were a weapon.

Jenna watched the play of emotions on his face and saw a sudden transforming smile light up his face.

"I'm so stupid," he said, handing her the key. *"In the hands of a maiden, young and pure will a key of bronze unlock a door,"* he said, reciting the verse they had found in the manuscript. "It will work only for you."

Jenna slipped the lovely decorative bronze key into the lock and with an indrawn breath and a whispered prayer, turned it, listening with a soaring heart as the tumblers clicked, and the lock came undone.

Aidan gave the door a hard push, and with a groan of an old man awakened from sleep, it opened into the deepening night.

"It smells like the ocean," was Jenna's immediate response. She breathed deeply, and in her mind's eye, saw waves lapping at a beach.

"Look there's a path." She pointed out a trail of broken stones leading away from the castle toward a grove of trees which were swaying in the wind. The rumble of thunder was louder, and the air was growing briskly colder, feeling like early winter, not late spring.

"And look behind you." Aidan turned Jenna to face into the castle. "Here's another door. This is it. This is the way to the dungeon, I'm sure of it."

Jenna tried not to think of the sisters' vivid descriptions of what lay beyond the door. "It will be so dark there," she muttered, her heart pounding.

"The flame looks like gold," Aidan replied softly.

She looked at her sea-treasure-turned-lantern. *It's like a golden dancing prayer.*

"Jenna, what am I to do?" Aidan's tone of voice suddenly changed, sounding much more like the boy he was, rather than The king he wished to be. "How can I let you go into such a dangerous place alone. To face that vile creature."

His tone grew anguished. "You're leaving, and I've only just begun to know you."

Jenna wanted to weep. Had she only known him a day? He was already a cherished friend, one she surely had known for years, and had only just been reunited with. Jenna's throat ached with suppressed sobs and her voice trembled as she said, "Daniel told me that our journeys bring us gifts we would never have received if we had never ventured forward."

She rushed the words to keep ahead of her gathering tears. "You—and the sisters—have been one of those unexpected gifts. And I know..." She stopped, struggling to find just the right words. "I know someday, in some other time or space, we will meet again."

Aidan's face was tortured with doubt and indecision.

"I know I can do this thing because of you, Aidan. I never would have discovered any of this on my own. So, now, please, go back where you will be safe. The time will come when you, too, are called on a journey. But now is not that time."

His words were fierce, angry. "Jenna, I can't, I won't leave you to do this alone."

She shook her head vigorously. "You know you must go. You have to be sure the sisters aren't punished because Genevieve is gone. Please, please..." She retrieved the dancing flame from the floor with one hand, and with her other pulled him back down the passage out into the chapel.

"Please, Aidan. Please. If you linger, I won't have the courage to go into that dungeon. Please go. Now. And take care of Joy, Innocence, Wonder, and Delight. Do this for me, please." She gave him a tiny push and heard his muffled groan as at first he resisted, then fled, his steps echoing in the deserted chapel.

When she heard Aidan close the chapel door behind him, her legs suddenly gave out, and she sank in a heap on the floor, fear twisting her stomach into a nauseous knot. Down in that dark, dank dungeon The Keeper awaited her.

"I cannot do this," she groaned. "I can't."

She pictured Daniel in Olmigira's cave, lost in sleep, awaiting her return.

"I'm sorry, Daniel, I can't!"

Her breath made a puff of cloud in the cold, damp chapel, and floated upward like incense.

An unexpected surge of rage rushed through her like a heated wave. "Why must I do this? Why? I won't, I tell you, I won't," she said, not knowing who she was raging at.

She flung her sea treasure away from her and dropped her head into her hands, all her fear, confusion, and anger pouring out in tears. Misery, longing, and defeat filled her soul. She cried for a very long time, until there were no more tears left. Exhausted, she huddled beneath her cloak in the bone-chilling dampness.

The silence of the soaring space slowly seeped into her awareness, and something aroused her. Some sound. Some sense. Some voice in her mind.

Daniel's voice.

Jenna, don't give up. She's been calling all these years. You're the only one who heard.

Lifting her head, she saw the sea-green bottle a short distance away on the stone floor, miraculously unbroken, sitting upright, its flame almost dying. With a gasp, she picked herself up and ran to it, lifting it to her face. As she did, the chapel became lighter and ahead, on the broken, crumbling altar she saw a mourning dove. Heard its quiet cooing.

As she watched, the bird took flight, circling around and around the chapel, higher and higher in graceful spirals, until it slipped through the broken rafters, out into the night sky. She pictured it soaring across the wheat field, over the woods and by the frozen pond, back the long distance to Olmigira's cave.

In her mind, she saw the dove landing next to Daniel, cooing its gentle, comforting song into his sleeping ear.

He won't wake up until I get back. I'll never get back if I don't go into the dungeon and release Genevieve.

She took in a lungful of air and breathed out the last of her resistance.

Then, on quick, sure steps she ran back through the passageway to the dungeon door. As she stood facing the barrier between her and Genevieve, the door in the western wall behind her swung back and forth in the growing wind. A crack of lighting flared, warning the storm was near.

Ahead of her, huge spider webs were her first challenge.

Ugh. Spiders. Of all nature's creatures, spiders were her least favorite. With a shutter, she scraped the webs from the door latch and pulled. The door swung open in eerie silence.

Holding the light in front of her, she stepped through onto a landing. Below her, the narrow, steep, circular steps descended into darkness.

"Does everything here have to lead around in circles?" she muttered aloud.

With each step downward, the damp air grew thicker and more putrid, full of the smell of rotting hope. The only light came from the dancing flame, which burned low and intensely. Round and round, down and down, the steps seemed endless.

How deep can the dungeon be? Wasn't it right beneath the chapel?

At last, she stepped out into a hallway that led to the left and right. Ahead of her, just as the girls had described in their story of visiting Genevieve, were several heavy wooden doors with barred openings. Which one was Genevieve's cell?

The answer came as low mournful weeping floated out on the air. It was the sound of unquenchable tears, of a heart wasting away with no one to grieve for its loss.

Jenna hurriedly took the key which hung on a nearby nail and unlocked the door on the left. As she pulled it open, the scent of decay flooded her nose, even as the dancing flame grew suddenly taller and began waving with grace and vigor.

The weeping stopped.

No light or windows broke the intense darkness below her. Only the scuffle of rodent feet interrupted the sudden silence. Where was The Keeper? The dancing flame caught her attention, and she recalled Aidan's words, "Near the dancing flame no vile or evil may approach." Her heart lightened.

By the glow of her lamp, she carefully descended the five steps into the airless cell. Ahead she could make out a thin, emaciated barefoot woman in a ragged, faded blue nightgown kneeling next to a stone pillar.

In a weak, trembling voice, the woman asked, "Are you a ghost? Why have you come?" She began to weep again. "It is too late. Jacob is lost. All are lost. I sent them to their deaths. I am condemned to mourn forever in the darkness."

Once again, the woman fell to keening her unearthly wail that curled along Jenna's spine and sucked the breath from her. *The Woman Who Wails in the Night.*

Jenna knelt beside the despondent woman whose bedraggled appearance tore at her heart.

Could this be my grandmother? It makes no sense. Yet the story this woman told the sisters matches what Aunt Myra told me about my father's mother.

"No, Genevieve, you've wept enough. I've come to set you free."

The woman lifted her head again. The flickering light shone on her dirt-streaked face and reflected in her bloodshot eyes. She blinked as if the brightness hurt them. "Free?"

"Yes."

Genevieve sat back on her legs, looking up at Jenna. "But why? How?" Sobs began to shake her body.

"No, no, do not weep any longer."

Setting the dancing flame on the floor, Jenna rested the woman's head against her heart and rocked from side to side. Some dizzying sense of familiarity, some memory stirred with each sway of her body. Yet how could that be? Jenna's father had only been a boy when his mother died.

As the woman's sobbing eased, Jenna said softly, "Genevieve?"

The frail woman slowly eased away from Jenna and looked directly at her.

In Genevieve's face, Jenna saw her father: that same quiet, waiting expression he often had in the same deep brown eyes. Jenna, stunned by the recognition, was speechless.

"Who are you?" Genevieve asked again, adding, "and why have you come?"

Jenna, more certain that this was truly her grandmother, answered the second question. "I've come to set you free." The sense of urgency rushed back through Jenna's veins. The Keeper was somewhere, lurking. "And we must hurry."

Genevieve trembled. "How can you unshackle me; the key is too high." She pointed higher up on the pillar. Jenna stood and stretched, but it was well beyond her reach.

She looked down at the prisoner. "You must boost me up."

"Boost you up?" The reply was incredulous. "I am too weak." Her limbs began to tremble. "I cannot." Genevieve's voice was full of self-pity.

Holding onto her courage, Jenna said as calmly as she could, "Don't you want to get out of here? You must help me in some way."

Genevieve began to moan. "I don't deserve it. This is what I deserve. To stay here forever. He owns my soul." She let out a loud, long wail.

Jenna, growing rapidly weary of the woman's tears, suspected that they were a way she had often gotten others to do her bidding. Exasperated, Jenna muttered, "Don't you do anything else except cry?"

The woman suddenly stood up, startling Jenna so much, she stepped back, wary.

"Of course, I can do things besides cry. I'm a sailor's wife. I've things to tend to."

Jenna sensed a spark of the Genevieve of years ago.

"Yes," Genevieve continued, "there are things to tend to. I don't have the strength to boost *you*, but if you wrap your arms around the post, I will climb you like a tree in the meadow and reach the keys."

Just then the dancing flame began to dance more vigorously.

The Keeper knows I'm here.

Jenna suddenly thought about the conversation with Olmigira about lost spirits. "Is there no way for such a spirit to be saved?" she had asked the old woman.

Olmigira had responded, "Sometimes a person of great courage can free that lost soul. But it requires a great price."

The Keeper can't come near the dancing flame, so I'm safe. But it will expect a great price.

As she tried to imagine what great price might be extracted, Jenna barely heard Genevieve who kept saying, "I'm ready; I'm ready,"

The nightmares...

Jenna trembled at the very thought of those nightmares. What if they never went away? What if every night, for the rest of her life, she would be drawn into that terrifying darkness where that faceless, hooded being would reach out to her with its skeletal hand.

The image of young Genevieve, finding treasures at the seashore, stepped into her mind. And of that little girl grown into a woman, left to spend an eternity in this foul place. Could she condemn that woman to such a fate?

Maybe I can learn to live with the terror. I'll still be able to go home, to see Mama and Papa and the boys. And I'll be able to waken Daniel. Maybe the nightmares will be tolerable because I'll know them for what they are.

"Girl, girl, have you no ears?" Genevieve's voice pierced her thoughts.

"Yes, yes, I'm ready," Jenna came alert and grabbed onto the pillar.

Using Jenna's body like the trunk of a tree, Genevieve stepped up onto her shoulders, reached high and grasped the key ring, then slithered back down Jenna's back to the floor.

The dancing flame leapt in response.

It's clapping, Jenna thought, the idea making her smile. She knelt, unlocking Genevieve's shackles from her ankles. The long-captured woman collapsed in a pile on the floor, weeping.

"There's no time for your wailing and guilt if we're to get out of here," Jenna said, as she shook Genevieve's shoulders.

But as Genevieve lifted her face, it was radiant, illuminated by the dancing flame. She was a gaunt beauty, a shadow of her former self, but Jenna could see why she had once turned heads. It was beyond logic or sense, but this was her grandmother. A woman who died when Jenna's father had been a little boy, long before Jenna herself was born.

Yet alive. Now. In front of her.

Jenna's mind reeled, yet her heart grew warm with the knowledge.

"You've done it," Genevieve said. "We've done it." The young woman laughed, nearly hysterical, transformed by the turn of a key.

Jenna bent to pick up the dancing flame, and urged, "Come, let us go."

With one hand cupping the sea-green bottle and the other gripping her grandmother's arm, Jenna led the way across the dungeon floor. As they were about to mount the first step, she felt something moving behind her and heard a rattling breath. An unnatural coldness began to seep into her body through her feet. A sound like a sneer of triumph echoed in her ear.

The Keeper.

12

AND DREAMS OF HOME

Spinning around, Jenna peered into the murky darkness of the dungeon, barely illuminated by the dancing flame. She could see no form, no substance, nothing to distinguish The Keeper from among the deep shadows of the cell.

But she could hear its breath, sense its presence.

To her relief, when she held the light higher, the breathing grew dimmer.

"He's afraid!" Genevieve's astounded words rang in Jenna's ears over the pounding beat of her heart. She heard triumph in Genevieve's voice.

"The Keeper is afraid!" She turned to look at Jenna. "Who are you?" she asked with awe.

Jenna felt woozy and weak and the hand holding the dancing flame trembled. As she turned once again to the stairs and reached out to help her grandmother, she said quickly, "No time now. I can explain later. First, let's get out of here."

Genevieve's burst of energy at discovering The Keeper was afraid of her rescuer waned quickly. She could barely make two steps without needing to lean against the wall. The climb to the passageway and then up the narrow winding steps to the door in the western wall was excruciatingly slow and exhausting for both of them.

All the while, Jenna tried to block out thoughts of the unseen presence behind her, but its hatred, bitterness, fury, and jealousy were like winged creatures biting at her.

When they finally reached the outer door, Jenna and Genevieve both sank to the floor, overcome. Ahead of them the door creaked on its hinges, to and fro, banging against the castle wall rhythmically in the wind.

The swirling clouds and streaks of lightning sent shards of fear into Jenna's heart.

Genevieve gasped. "It's a wicked night. The storm…"

"Rest a moment, but we must go west," Jenna replied.

To the west is the sea, wide and deep.

Genevieve shook her head, vehemently. "I'm afraid of the sea. I can't go back there."

"We must go to the west!" Jenna said, alarmed at her grandmother's protest. It hadn't occurred to her that her grandmother would refuse.

Genevieve suddenly dissolved into tears. "No, I must sleep. I'm so tired. I've been weeping for years. I don't want to go to the sea; I don't want to remember anymore. Just allow me the sleep of forgetfulness."

Jenna knew Genevieve had to reach the edge of the ocean. It was there her journey had begun as a little girl playing in the sand and dancing with the waves, and it was there she must return.

A circle. In the end, we come back to where we started.

"I think something important will happen if we go to the sea," Jenna urged. "We must hurry, because I don't know if the dancing flame will go out in the wind."

Her worried voice penetrated Genevieve's weeping.

"The dancing flame?" Genevieve looked more closely at the bottle. Her eyes grew wide. "What is this bottle? It shines so... sea-green."

Jenna held the globe out to her grandmother who took it in her hands and stared at it, eyes wide with fear. "But I buried it. In the sand. That night by the sea. In the storm. After little Joanna..."

Genevieve pulled away from Jenna. "Who are you? Where did you get this?" Her tone was insistent, although her voice quavered.

"I found it in the sand in a tide pool. Near Westerfordshire." Jenna tried to get Genevieve to her feet, but the young woman resisted. "If I tell you who I am, will you promise me that we can go toward the sea?" Jenna tried not to watch the swirling clouds turning the sky a sickening green.

"Yes!"

Jenna sighed with frustration. "My name is Jenna. I live in the hill country a day's travel east of Westerfordshire. I have three older brothers—Joshua, Abram, and Thomas; and one younger brother, Peter."

Jenna felt Genevieve's unspoken impatience.

"But why are you here?"

Jenna heard her own question come from her grandmother's mouth.

"My mother's name is Rachel. And my father..." Jenna felt her throat constrict. How she missed him. "My father's name is Jacob."

She heard Genevieve's in-drawn breath.

"He grew up in Westerfordshire. His father was a sailor and his mother's name is..."

"Genevieve. Genevieve Regina." Jenna's grandmother completed the sentence. She looked at Jenna, blinking her rheumy eyes, shaking her head in disbelief. "You're my Jacob's daughter."

"Yes," Jenna agreed softly. "I am."

The bedraggled young woman reached out a hand to Jenna's cheek. "I haven't been forgotten. That girl who came into the dungeon—she said in my dreams I would find someone. I kept calling. I knew that if Jacob grew up and married, he would name his daughter after me. So I kept calling. You heard me."

Genevieve's voice grew stronger. "I thought that maybe if there is someone who still remembered me, I could yet be forgiven. You said we need to go to the sea? Yes, yes. The sea where I wished... where I... Yes, yes, you're right. I can smell the salt air. It must be this way."

Genevieve stumbled to her feet, then stepped out into the wildly windy night.

Jenna followed, taking the dancing flame from her grandmother's hand, and leading the way. As they moved away from the shelter of the castle, the flickering fire had to fight harder for its life.

Would The Keeper catch them if the flame died? Jenna drew her cloak around the front of the bottle, which she held close to her body to protect it from the wind.

"Genevieve," her grandmother said, calling her by her given name, the way a grandmother would, "the light! Genevieve Regina, we need the light. Do not hoard it close to yourself."

"But Grandmére, it will go out if I do not shelter it."

"Genevieve," her grandmother's voice drifted to her on the wind, "the dancing flame has a life of its own."

With reluctance, Jenna lifted the sea-green bottle to shoulder height. The path ahead was again lit with a golden glow. Although the flame danced ferociously against the wind, it did not go out. Jenna breathed a sigh of relief.

In a few steps, she was at the edge of the moat, a wide ribbon of brackish water bound by two ledges of rock.

"A bridge, there must be a bridge," Genevieve was muttering.

Jenna reached inside her pinafore and brought out Aidan's map.

"Here, help me shelter it from the wind so we can read it." They huddled over the map, their bodies a shield.

"The path leads to the moat and to a bridge which crosses it," Genevieve said, pointing to the map. "But where is the bridge? We are here at the end of the path. Maybe it was destroyed in a storm. Maybe The Keeper…" She shivered at his name.

"I'll walk along the moat a bit, and see if I can find it," Jenna said, raising her voice to make herself heard over the increasing volume of the wind. The trees along the moat were swaying with abandon and the bursts of lightning coming more rapidly. But though she paced some distance in one direction and then the other, she found nothing.

"Here's where the path came down from the castle," Genevieve pointed out. "The bridge should be right here. See, the path continues on the other side." She pointed across the water in the moat, which was about ten feet wide.

"Wait!" Jenna looked at Genevieve. "I've an idea."

Drawing off her slippers and stockings and tucking them in her pinafore pockets, she held the dancing flame over her head.

"What, what are you doing?" her grandmother shrieked, reaching for Jenna as she sat down on the stone rim of the moat.

Jenna ignored her. Reaching into the water with her feet, she stretched down as far as she could without slipping off the bank. When the water was almost to her knees, she felt something solid. Stone.

"It's here. The bridge is here, underneath the surface of the water." She shivered in the cold. It was impossible to hold up her pinafore and the bottle. She let her dress drop into the water and stood up. The stone was icy cold and slippery, but solid.

"Come, come, it's this way." She took several steps through the swirling water, then looked back at her grandmother. "What's wrong? Come!"

Genevieve looked at her forlornly. "I cannot swim."

"You do not have to swim—merely walk," Jenna replied, frustrated with her grandmother's constant excuses.

"But I may slip off into the deep water." The young woman was trembling, but not with cold. "I would drown." A haunted look came to her face.

"Do not slip off then," Jenna said with impeccable logic, the kind that would have made Aidan proud.

With fear-filled eyes, Genevieve slowly sat on the edge of the bank and eased herself into the water. She stretched her hand out to Jenna, who stood sideways on the submerged bridge, her right hand holding the lantern, her left hand reaching back to Genevieve.

Ever so slowly, they eased their way through the icy moat, fighting to keep their balance in the bitter cold and choppy water. When they scrambled up the other side, they both collapsed, exhausted and freezing.

"We must keep moving," Jenna urged. "We cannot let the cold overcome us."

She hurriedly put her stockings and shoes back on. Her dress was sopping from her knees down, the wetness slowly wicking upward. Stumbling, they rose and went forward. The air smelled more strongly of sea salt.

"Aidan said the land is marshy, and we must stick to the path for there are dangerous bogs," Jenna shouted over the wind as she huddled under a swaying tree, trying to read the map which she had again taken from her pinafore.

"The map shows the road going to the left at a fork ahead," Genevieve said through chattering teeth.

Jenna folded the map and put it back inside her dress. Taking the older woman's hand, she said, "Come, it can't be far."

But it was.

They walked on, shivering in the cold wind, their damp clothing chilling them to the bones. Jenna felt her legs grow numb. She had no sense of distance or time, only that the way seemed endless. At last they found the fork in the road. By then the rain had begun to fall, pelting them with icy-cold splinters.

Jenna plodded ahead, trying to ignore the painfully aching chill.

I wish I were in Olmigira's cave where it was warm.

She heard Genevieve behind her, struggling to catch her breath.

The path took a turn up an incline and suddenly Jenna heard the sound of breakers in the distance. Slipping and falling constantly, they worked their way up the hill. As they ascended to the top, the raging roar of the ocean suddenly filled Jenna's ears.

In the west, a thin ribbon of fading light stretched over the sea, which was dashing itself against rocks at the edge of a bay that lay in an arc before them. The storm, moving in from the east, was rapidly overtaking the western horizon.

Genevieve moaned. "No, I can't." She turned back in the direction of the castle.

Jenna grabbed her. "What's wrong with you? We're almost there."

Genevieve turned to face Jenna. In the light of the dancing flame, Jenna saw that the bedraggled prisoner had undergone an amazing transformation. The gaunt, wasted face had been replaced by a young woman's delicate, beautiful one. Her eyes were clear and lucid, free of tears, but filled with anguish.

"It was here, here that he drowned," she said, pointing to the shoals. "It was here I watched the ship go down. It was here I stood and spared not a shred of pity for the others who drowned with him."

Jenna knew her grandmother had not seen Jacob's ship go down, for she had lain on her deathbed in Westerfordshire.

Genevieve shook her head at Jenna. "I know what you are thinking—that it was a fevered dream. But my dying wish was that his mistress, the sea, would take him to her bosom. I remember standing here—on this dune—as I watched the ship go down. On a night like this."

She looked to the swirling clouds, green with jealousy, and the blue-black sea, raging with anger. "I stood here in the pouring rain; it was cold, cold, like this. I saw his ship break up on the rocks. I heard the screams of the men. I could have stopped it."

Jenna shook her head. "No, no, that's not possible. How could you? Even if you were here on the shore and not in a fevered dream. They were there, in the sea. It was not possible for you to save them or to stop the shipwreck. You were help-less."

She's so beautiful. She wouldn't have wished for such evil.

Jenna saw sadness and something else in her grandmother's eyes.

Shame.

"Oh, little Genevieve Regina, I was so full of anger. I blamed him, you see. I could not bear to believe it was my fault that Joanna died."

"Maybe it was no one's fault!" Jenna protested. "Maybe it was just to be!" She looked at her grandmother's grief-lined face.

"Perhaps. Perhaps. But don't you see, I wished it with my dying breath, and The Keeper granted my desire. He stood beside me on this hill, and I did not cry out for him to stop it."

Jenna was revolted at the thought of anyone making a bargain with that evil thing which so haunted her dreams.

"The Keeper said he would grant my wish, but because Jacob's soul and the souls of all the other men would be out of his reach, he would exact a great price."

The wind threw Genevieve's words back at them, taunting them. "A great price."

Jenna couldn't look at her grandmother. She could not comprehend how this woman, her father's mother, could have done such a thing, even as her grandmother said, "I said I was willing to pay. I did not even ask what the price was."

The wind reached a fevered pitch, battering them as they stood on the sandy dune. Genevieve's voice was almost as feverish.

"And what was it? The price? I learned it too late. It was to be locked away in darkness. Forgotten by everyone who ever knew I existed. Doomed to remember over and over again his sweet kisses, his laughing eyes, and my heart, broken every time he left me."

Jenna wanted to cover her ears and stop the sound of her grandmother's voice.

"And Joanna, to see her, night after night, just out of reach, asleep in the cradle. And my little boy, Jacob. To remember it all and have none of it. That was the price I've paid. But even if I had known the price, do you think that would have stopped me? I was so full of hatred... "

Genevieve turned to Jenna. She reached out and gently stroked Jenna's cheek, wet from the rain. "So now you see, little one—my Genevieve Regina, named for your grandmother—why I said I do not deserve freedom, why I do not deserve to be forgiven."

Jenna jerked away from her grandmother's touch. Driven by a need to get beyond her grandmother's reach, she ran down the dune onto the flat plain of the shore, her thoughts swirling more wildly than the clouds overhead or the sea before her.

What sorrow had been wrought by this one woman's wish for revenge: a boy, losing his mother, lost his father as well; grandchildren, never to know of their heritage; and she, Jenna, haunted by dreams of that Dark Presence, never-ending nightmares of a clawing terror that compelled her parents to find a reason, a cure, a solution.

Were the dreams Genevieve's fault too?

She whirled to find that her grandmother had followed her to the ocean's edge. She stood near, watching, waiting.

A sniveling thought insinuated itself into Jenna's mind.

I could leave her to The Keeper. He would drag her back to the dungeon and give me my freedom in exchange. I could go home. She deserves an eternity in that putrid cell for all the pain she has caused others. Why should I help her?

Jenna knew her grandmother was aware of her thoughts and silently, listlessly awaited her judgment.

Jenna trembled with the power she held. The power to punish. The power to withhold forgivingness. Her grandmother hadn't forgiven Jenna's grandfather for his love of the sea. Why should she forgive her grandmother for calling her out of her life into this nameless place?

The world seemed to stand still for a moment, holding its breath, as if waiting for Jenna to decide. Jenna held her breath as well, waiting for an answer, for illumination.

She looked at the flame in her grandmother's sea-green bottle as it flickered and danced as if full of joy.

Letting out her breath slowly, Jenna turned to face the wind.

"No," she shouted at the wind. "No," she shouted at the sea. "No," she shouted at the rain. "I won't let him win. I won't send her back."

The sky, the sea, the wind seemed to suddenly pause as if to listen, to hear her words.

Turning to Genevieve, who had come to stand beside her, Jenna said, "I am your granddaughter. I don't know if you sent the dark dreams. I don't believe you would or could. I believe you did call me across the years. I have been called here, not to send you back into the darkness, but to give you the light that someone gave to me."

The specter of darkness lurked behind them just over the hill. Jenna knew if she gave away the light, her nightmares might haunt her always, even in the midst of day.

"The legend says, near the dancing flame, no vile or evil can draw near. You will be protected, safe." Jenna heard her own voice choking, but felt no sorrow, no pain, only a deep, unfathomable rightness in what she was about to do.

Silently, she offered the dancing flame to her grandmother in a "yes" as deep as the ocean.

Genevieve's beautiful face filled with astonishment. With trembling hands, she took the dancing flame, the sea-treasure that she herself had found so many, many years ago. For a moment she looked down at the iridescent bottle, then out to the ocean.

Her face aglow with gratitude, she walked toward the sea, which, along with the sky, had turned suddenly still, as if they too were holding their breath, waiting to see what Genevieve would do.

The only sounds that filled the night's silence were the soft waves washing the beach—each lap receding.

"It's to be low tide soon," Genevieve said to the sea, as she gently set the bottle with its dancing flame on the water. It bobbed gracefully on the tiny ripples. "Take this to my Jacob, so no vile or evil thing will be able to draw near to him."

The sea, in obedience, took back the treasure it had once given her, when she was young and innocent. Jenna stood by her grandmother watching the bottle slowly float out to sea.

As the bottle grew smaller and smaller in the distance, the clouds, once green with jealousy, thinned and weakened. Stars began to peek through. In a short time, the sky cleared.

Overhead, a thousand pinpricks of light shone down from a thousand worlds beyond imagining. The stars seemed to be watching as the sea-given treasure aflame with the fire of love was swept out to sea by the tide, eventually lost to sight.

For a very long time, a time too long to measure, Jenna and her grandmother looked out to sea. A warm breeze began to dry their clothes. Though the dancing flame was gone, Jenna felt no fear.

The Keeper's gone into hiding, at least for now.

Jenna and Genevieve sat down on the beach, wrapped in Jenna's cloak, and listened to the song of the sea, heard its waltz, breathed its rhythm. As women have done for countless generations, they looked out to sea and waited for those they love to come home.

With the first hint of dawn in the east behind them, Jenna saw a man walking down the shoreline from the north. As he drew closer and the light grew brighter, she saw by his clothes that he was a sailor. Jenna watched as the man drew nearer, and saw the fearful, hopeful anticipation on her grandmother's face.

When he was just a half dozen paces from them, Genevieve leapt to her feet and cried out the answer to Jenna's unspoken question.

"Jacob!"

The beautiful young wife ran with joyful steps into the waiting arms of her husband, come home from the sea.

Jenna saw her grandmother's look of joy beyond measure and her grandfather's smile of astonished happiness. They turned toward her, gratitude, love, and redemption shining from their eyes. The grandfather Jenna had never met smiled a shy, gentle hello, so much like his son Jacob's, that Jenna nearly lost her composure. She longed to throw her arms around him and tell him how proud he would be of his son.

There were no words needed. Everything that needed to be said was said by their hearts.

That her willingness to answer a desperate voice in her dreams had enabled this improbable, impossible reunion to happen filled Jenna with inexpressible joy.

With one final nod of acknowledgement, the couple turned and walked away down the beach, hand-in-hand, heading south, growing smaller and smaller in the distance until she could see them no more.

Jenna was suddenly overcome with fatigue.

With a trembling sigh of exhaustion, she lay down on the sand, curled up on her side facing the ocean. Resting her head on her arms, she covered herself with her cloak.

As the sun peeped over the eastern horizon behind her, filling the world with light, she closed her eyes, falling softly into sleep.

And dreamed of home.

THE END

The story continues in Book 2: The Boy in the Tower

ACKNOWLEDGEMENTS

Like many young adult fantasies, *The Bronze Key* can be read on two levels. The first level is pure story: a young girl on the verge of womanhood takes a treacherous journey to face an evil presence that haunts her dreams. In the process she answers a desperate call for help across time and distance from a long ago world where the seasons have been frozen. The second level is a metaphor for the inner journey many young people and adults take—the journey to face dark memories or personal wounds that are buried in their subconscious.

Both are stories of personal bravery.

In times of great world turmoil, readers of all ages need examples of heroines and heroes of all ages who, despite great fear and even physical danger, muster up their courage and step forward to face inner demons or outward evil. And even more, to make the incredibly difficult decision to forgive those who have caused them great harm and deep pain.

I originally wrote the four books of Jenna's Journey in the 1990s following the death of my mother, as I was trying to come to grips with questions I wished I had asked her was she was still living. The manuscripts were then put aside and I went on to write other stories, including *The Bomber Jacket*, a World War II ghost story, which was published in August 2024.

Shortly after *The Bomber Jacket* was accepted by Wild Ink Publishing, I submitted *The Bronze Key* for consideration, and to my astonishment, they said they loved it. In three months I had signed two book contracts for stories which have been quietly waiting for their time to take their journey into the world.

Many thanks to all of the Wild Ink team who saw the value in this story and put in the intense hours of work to bring it to print: Abigail Wild, Brittany McMunn, Laura Wackwitz and the other Wild Ink staff for so much behind-the-scenes work.

Special thanks to Jordie, whose healing experiences of guided imagery revealed the first hint of this story to me and started me on this writing journey. To Peg, who has nourished me along the path. And to Dana, my husband, who has loved me every inch of the way.

With special thanks to: Sandy, whose Still Waters Retreat House by the Conodoguinet Creek gave me sacred space for writing; to my fellow Gemeinschaft sojourners at the Lititz Moravian Church, who affirmed my call to write; and to my children, Michelle and Benjamin, who have kept me young at heart.

K.M. King lives with her husband Dana in Lancaster County, Pennsylvania. They have two children and four grandchildren. Her career includes work in journalism, public education, staff development, county social services, management training, and personal coaching. She is a veteran of the United States Army.

She is the author of *The Bomber Jacket,* a World War II ghost story, also published by Wild Ink Publishing, and two journaling workbooks: *Pen, Power and Possibilities: A Guided Journaling Experience to Expand the Horizons of Your Life* and

Time: Tyrant or Treasure—11 Steps to Embracing Life in All Its Messiness.

She enjoys playing scrabble, wandering around museums, dabbling in abstract art, writing poetry, engaging in philosophical discussions, and listening to K-pop, especially BTS. Her blog, *Kdrama for Life*, views life through the lens of Kdrama.

Learn about K.M. King's upcoming works, purchase her journaling workbooks, and connect to her blogs at her website: www.kmkingauthor.com.